"Best friends, bargain hunting, and murder! This new cozy mystery series has great promise and I'm looking forward to seeing what the bargain-hunting babes of St. Stanley will be up to next."
                                                    —*Novel Reflections*

"This author knows how to engage the reader's interest. Good, solid writing, well-formed characters, an enjoyable premise, a possible romance in the making, and a mystery that slowly unfolds its secrets. A bargain read for sure!"
                                                    —*Once Upon a Romance*

"What an enjoyable read! I loved the spunky Maggie."
                                                    —*Two Lips Reviews*

"The Good Buy Girls love a good deal—and a good murder . . . The debut of an all-new mystery series—and it's worth every penny."   —*I Dream Books*

"*50% off Murder* successfully launches a new series filled with a terrific cast of characters. It's a treat to see a mature group of women use their knowledge of the town and their business skills to look for a killer. And, Maggie is a wonderful amateur sleuth . . . 100% captivating and enjoyable."
                                                    —*Lesa's Book Critiques*

"An entertaining cozy starring interesting characters . . . Readers will admire [Maggie's] risk-taking spunk and enjoy the sparks between her and the sheriff."
                                                    —*The Mystery Gazette*

"With some interesting characters and a unique theme, this series is sure to be a hit!"   —*Debbie's Book Bag*

"Readers who want a laugh-out-loud mystery should enjoy *50% off Murder.*"   —*West Orlando News Online*

Buried in Bargains

Josie Belle

BERKLEY PRIME CRIME, NEW YORK

THE BERKLEY PUBLISHING GROUP
Published by the Penguin Group
Penguin Group (USA) LLC
375 Hudson Street, New York, New York 10014, USA

USA I Canada I UK I Ireland I Australia I New Zealand I India I South Africa I China

Penguin Books Ltd., Registered Offices: 80 Strand, London WC2R 0RL, England
For more information about the Penguin Group, visit penguin.com.

BURIED IN BARGAINS

A Berkley Prime Crime Book / published by arrangement with the author

Berkley Prime Crime Books are published by The Berkley Publishing Group.
BERKLEY® PRIME CRIME and the PRIME CRIME logo are trademarks
of Penguin Group (USA) LLC.

For information, address: The Berkley Publishing Group,
a division of Penguin Group (USA) LLC.
375 Hudson Street, New York, New York 10014.

ISBN: 978-0-425-25230-7

PUBLISHING HISTORY
Berkley Prime Crime mass-market edition / October 2013

PRINTED IN THE UNITED STATES OF AMERICA

10 9 8 7 6 5 4 3 2 1

Cover illustration by Mary Ann Lasher.
Cover design by Sarah Oberrender.
Interior text design by Laura K. Corless.

ALWAYS LEARNING   **PEARSON**

For my bargain-hunting buddy and dear friend Christina. Coffee and shopping dates with you are always full of belly-cramping laughs and lovely girl talk. I treasure the time we spend together. I love you, Sweetie!

Chapter 1

"Mom, you need to get a grip," Laura Gerber said to her mother as they trudged up the sidewalk through the center of St. Stanley, Virginia. "Summer Phillips is not worth getting an ulcer over."

"I'm not getting an ulcer," Maggie said. She noted that the small town was still quiet with very few people out in the chilly December morning temperatures.

Maggie glanced at her daughter, who was home from college for the holidays. Laura looked remarkably like Maggie had when she was twenty years old, with the same wrinkle-free face, shoulder-length red hair and upturned nose. Only the eyes were different. Where Maggie had green eyes, Laura had gotten her father's chocolate-brown eyes.

Maggie felt a pang, wishing her late husband, Charlie, could see their daughter now. She had grown up to be a smart, confident and beautiful young woman. Maggie couldn't have been more proud of her.

"Yeah, right, no ulcer," Laura said. "That's why you're popping antacid tablets like they're Pez."

Maggie stuffed the roll of tablets back into her purse. "Let's just focus on the mission, shall we?"

"Mission?" Laura asked and laughed. "I think you and the rest of the Good Buy Girls missed your calling."

"Meaning?" Maggie asked.

"You should really be military strategists," she said. "I've never seen such an organized assault for bargains."

"It's our gift," Maggie said with a smile. "Now, we have to hurry. We need to get to the stationery store as soon as they open. Janice Truman is selling last year's gift wrap at seventy-five percent off, and I want to stock up so we can offer free gift wrapping at My Sister's Closet."

"Yes, yes, I know," Laura said. "Do you really think customers will go to your resale shop instead of Summer's Second Time Around just because of free gift wrap?"

"If they have any taste they will," Maggie said. "Did you see the hideous window display she has up? Giant cardboard cutouts of herself dressed in a slutty Santa's helper outfit. Honestly, the woman has no sense of decency."

"Don't tell me. Let me guess," Ginger Lancaster said as she joined them at the corner. "We're talking about Summer's holiday window display."

"Revolting," Joanne Claramotta said as she stepped out from in front of her husband's deli, More than Meats, and joined their group. "I saw Tyler Fawkes standing in front of her store for about twenty minutes yesterday. I swear he would have licked the glass if he weren't afraid of being seen."

"Ew," the others said in unison.

"See? It isn't just me," Maggie said to Laura.

Laura rolled her eyes. "Where's Claire?"

"She's meeting us in front of the shop," Ginger said. "She has to get to the library as soon as we're done."

Claire Freemont was the fourth member of the Good Buy Girls, a self-named club of bargain hunters, of which Maggie and Ginger were the longest-serving members. Best friends since they were toddlers, Maggie and Ginger had grown up in St. Stanley and settled down to raise their families there. When they began having children, both had become avid bargain hunters and had started the money-saving club together.

Write On, Janice's stationery store, was housed in a large brick building just off the town square. Maggie and her entourage turned the corner to Janice's shop just in time to see Claire Freemont going nose to nose with Summer Phillips.

"Darn it! I knew I should have camped out last night," Maggie said.

"Mom, seventy-five-percent-off wrapping paper is no reason to camp on a sidewalk," Laura said. "It's not like tickets to Springsteen."

"Michael would kill for tickets to Springsteen," Joanne said.

"Focus, people, focus," Maggie said. "We're thinking about wrapping paper, bows and tags right now, not hot sixty-year-olds who can still slide across the stage on their knees."

"I watched that on YouTube like ten times," Ginger said. Then she fanned herself with one hand. " 'Waitin' on a Sunny Day,' indeed."

Maggie gave her a quelling look. "As I was saying, look out for the cheesy paper that rips easily; we want the foil or reversible paper. Remember, we're going for quality here."

"Summer, I was here first," Claire snapped. "You need to quit crowding me."

"I'm not crowding you." Summer tossed her long blonde locks. "You're just fat."

Ginger hissed in a breath through her teeth. She looked like she was gearing up to do some damage to Summer, who was tall and skinny with abnormally large frontal lobes— no, not the ones in her brain. Maggie put her hand on Ginger's arm.

"Out-shopping her will be the best revenge," she said.

Ginger adjusted the bright blue knitted cap she wore on her close-cropped hair. Her dark brown skin was flushed with temper, but she gave Maggie a nod.

"Fine. Just stay between me and her," she said.

"I can do that," Joanne said with a flick of her long brown ponytail.

Joanne was six months pregnant and had finally started to show. It had taken her a long time to get pregnant, and she was so excited, she had started wearing maternity clothes on the day she made the announcement. Maggie was pleased to see that Joanne's clothes were finally fitting her gently rounded belly.

"Now, if there is a ruckus, you and the baby skedaddle," Ginger said. "Maggie and Laura can run interference."

En masse they approached the front door, where Claire and Summer were jostling elbows.

Claire spotted them and sent them a beaming smile.

Maggie knew Claire must have been relieved to have her posse arrive just in time to save her from the bully.

Summer followed Claire's gaze and her eyes locked onto Maggie and then shifted to Laura.

"Oh god, there's two of you," she said. "Because one wasn't bad enough."

For some reason this delighted Maggie and she threw her arm around Laura and hugged her close.

"Double the fun," she said.

Summer's lip curled back, "More like a double hernia."

Laura glanced between them and frowned.

"Don't you think you two should get over this? You're both women in business, you need to work together not tear each other apart. If women were more supportive of one another, instead of always shredding each other over their appearances or a man's attention, we'd be getting a lot further in the world than having women make up only three percent of the CEOs in the United States."

Summer and Maggie looked at her and then at each other, and then they both shook their heads.

"Normally, I would agree with you," Maggie began, but Summer interrupted.

"The truth is that your mother has never gotten over the fact that I stole her high school boyfriend. It's a pity, because I really think we could have been friends, you know, if she wasn't so jealous of me," Summer said. The she turned back to the glass front door and started examining her reflection.

"Argh," Maggie growled. She wasn't aware that she had reached out to grab a fistful of Summer's blonde extensions until Ginger smacked her hand away.

"Out-shop her, remember?" she hissed.

Maggie's growl became a low rumble in her throat. She knew she should let it go, but somehow she just couldn't.

"Laura, dear," she began, "just so we're clear. I was dating a very nice boy back in high school and, yes, I did think that Summer had hooked up with him, but it turned out she had gotten another boy to wear my boyfriend's football jersey to trick me into thinking he was cheating on me."

"Ah!" Laura gasped. "That's vile."

"Oh no, that's nothing," Maggie said. "Seeing Summer buck naked—now that was vile."

Summer whirled around and glared daggers at Maggie while Ginger snorted trying to keep from laughing. Maggie saw Janice, approaching to unlock the door. Knowing she could lure Summer away from the door, she took a step back. Summer followed, just like Maggie had known she would.

"Why you—" Summer began, but Maggie interrupted her.

"What?" Maggie said, stepping back from the others. Again, Summer followed and Maggie watched as the GBGs closed ranks on the door. "Did you really think Sam and I wouldn't figure it out?"

"Oh, so you admit that you are 'Sam and I' now," Summer said. "Do not tell me that fabulous hunk of man is interested in you again."

Maggie maintained eye contact with Summer, but she could see over her shoulder that the door had opened and the GBGs had filed into the shop.

"It's none of your business," Maggie said.

"Oh, please," Summer said. "Your shop is right across the street from mine. Do you honestly think I haven't noticed that Sam stops by your shop regularly? What is going on between you two?"

"He's the sheriff. He's just doing his job," Maggie said. Now that the girls were in the shop, she didn't want to be out here in the cold debating her love life with Summer. "Oh, look at that!"

She scuttled around Summer toward the shop. She knew Summer was going to have a fit, and she braced herself to be taken out at the knees.

"Oh!" Summer cried as she hurried to catch up to her. "You distracted me on purpose."

"You think?" Maggie asked.

Summer's longer stride overtook Maggie, and she gave Maggie a hearty shove to the side. Maggie let her. She trusted her peeps to have already scored the good stuff, leaving the dreck for Summer.

"I loathe you, Maggie Gerber!" Summer cried as she yanked open the door and stormed into the shop. The door slammed in Maggie's face, and she smiled. The feeling was entirely mutual.

"Maggie, what are you up to now?" a voice asked from behind her.

Maggie turned around and felt her chest get tight. Speak of the devil. Sheriff Sam Collins was standing behind her with his arms crossed over his chest and a small smile playing on his lips.

Chapter 2

"Hi, Sam," Maggie said. She was pleased that her voice gave no indication of the tap dance her insides were doing at the sight of him. It had been twenty-plus years since they'd been a couple, but still the man made her dizzy. That could not be normal. "What makes you think I'm up to anything?"

"As soon as Della Harris saw you walk by her bookstore with the GBGs toward the same place Summer had just gone, she called the station," he said.

"No way," she said.

"Way," he said. "You and Summer do have a reputation, you know."

"It's not me," Maggie protested. "It's her."

Sam rolled his eyes.

"It is," Maggie protested.

"So, what's the deal du jour?" he asked.

"Seventy-five-percent-off wrapping paper."

"And you're out here instead of in there because . . . ?"

"The GBGs went in while I was exchanging . . . er . . . greetings with Summer."

Sam stepped closer to her and studied her with one eyebrow raised. "You didn't give her a black eye or anything, did you?"

"No!" Not that it wasn't tempting to take a swing at big, blonde and mean, but Maggie prided herself on her self-control.

Sam looked Maggie over in her black wool coat and olive green scarf. Her scarf had come loose, and he lifted one end and looped it around her head, adjusting it about her neck to keep her warm.

Maggie had the sudden urge to lean into him, but she found she couldn't move when he stood this close to her. The smoky citrus smell of his cologne made her inhale deeply, as if she could trap his scent inside of her.

"You look pretty today," he said. Then he gave her a smile hot enough to melt icicles. "Then again, you look pretty every day."

Maggie felt her face flame hot. Sam was flirting with her! Gone was her usual ability to verbally spar with him. She felt as if her tongue were stuck to the roof of her mouth like she'd just eaten a peanut butter sandwich. As if he knew this, he grinned and his eyes crinkled in the corners while dimples bracketed his smile.

"See you around, Maggie," he said, and he winked at her.

Maggie stood staring after him until he rounded the corner. What was she going to do with that man? Since he had confessed a month ago that he still cared about her and not just as a friend, she'd had no idea how to deal with him. Did he mean it? Was he just playing with her, trying to get her guard down? She didn't know.

There had been an evening a while back where she and the GBGs had been in Maggie's shop prepping for her big opening. They'd spotted Pete Daniels, who owned the local coffee shop, the Daily Grind, and Sam both headed toward her shop carrying flowers. Given that Maggie had just been released from the hospital, the girls had deduced that they were both bringing flowers for her. They had been wrong.

Pete had arrived at her shop with his peach-colored roses and a hug of sympathy for what she had been through. He had asked her to dinner previously, just as friends, so Maggie wasn't surprised by the gesture. Sam and his calla lilies had never arrived, so Maggie had figured the calla lilies had been for someone else. She had never found out who the lucky girl was. It had left Maggie in the awkward position of putting Pete off while she tried to figure what was happening between her and Sam, because even though Pete had said dinner was just as friends, she had the feeling it had been more than that. Was Sam seeing someone else? He certainly seemed to be in a better mood these days. Her usual pipeline into the local gossip had been sadly lacking in information on their handsome sheriff.

In the meantime, Sam seemed to turn up regularly at her shop, and he was always charming, but he never broached the subject of them being more than friends again. Maggie wondered if perhaps he was over her once and for all and really did just view her as a friend he could tease and flirt with, a friend who was safe. The thought was depressing.

The door to the stationery shop burst open and out poured the GBGs, each of them carrying an armload of wrapping paper. Maggie shook her head, dispelling thoughts of Sam, and focused on her friends.

"Foil, reversible, and Janice threw in two spools of matching ribbon," Claire said, holding out her bag for inspection. The others did the same, and Maggie was pleased with the haul. This would make it more than cost-effective for her to offer free gift wrap.

"You are a cheater, Maggie Gerber!" Summer shouted from the front door. "A big, fat sneaky cheater! I'll get you yet."

"I don't know what you're talking about," Maggie said, careful to keep her face neutral. "Happy shopping!"

"Oh, shove it up your chimney!" Summer bellowed, and slammed the door shut.

They were all silent for just a moment until Laura let out a giggle and the rest began to snicker, too, causing Joanne to bust out laughing. Claire looped her arm through Joanne's and dragged her away with the others following as they hurried back to Maggie's shop.

Laura helped Maggie set up her window display, advertising the free gift wrap with any purchase. They chose a big square box that they wrapped in gold foil and then used a green velvet ribbon as an accent. Laura came up with the idea to prop open the top of the box and put the free gift wrap message inside the lid.

It was just after lunch when Sandy, Maggie's niece, and her three-year-old son, Josh, dropped by the shop.

"Auntie Maggie!" Josh cried as he raced in the front door and ran across the shop to her.

Maggie turned and opened her arms, scooping Josh up into a warm hug. He had just turned three, and she was sure he had grown at least an inch since she'd seen him at break-fast that morning. She planted a kiss on his blond head and set him back down.

"How's my big guy?" she asked.

"We saw a train," he said. His eyes were huge, as if he was still enthralled by what he had seen.

"Where?" she asked him.

"Hammer store," he said. Maggie looked over his head to find Sandy smiling.

"Hardware store," Sandy explained. "They put up a huge Christmas display with a miniature village and several model trains that they have running nonstop. I really thought we were going to be there all day."

"Oh, I love those little villages," Maggie said. "I'll have to go and check it out."

"Now?" Josh asked hopefully. "We go now?"

"Auntie Maggie has to stay in her shop," Sandy said.

"She does, but I don't," Laura said. She knelt down on Josh's level, and asked, "Do you want to show me the trains?"

"Yes, yes, yes," Josh said, and he jumped up and down. "And maybe we'll see Santa."

Sandy gave him a worried look. "Josh, we talked about that."

He looked at his mother with such stubborness that Maggie raised her eyebrows and smiled at her niece.

"Oh, wow," she said. "Sandy, you looked just like that when you were three and determined to get your way. You about drove your mother crazy."

"Remind me to send her a sympathy card," Sandy said with a sigh.

"What's the trouble?" Maggie asked while Laura led Josh over to the little play area Maggie had set up in the corner of the shop to occupy kids who came shopping with their moms.

Sandy let out a sad sigh. "He wants to ask Santa to bring his dad home. I've explained to him that his dad is a soldier and he can't just up and leave Afghanistan, but Josh has his heart set on asking Santa. Ugh, I don't want the magic of the holidays to be ruined for him because Santa can't grant his wish."

"Oh, sweetie," Maggie gave her niece a hug. "I'm sorry. That is a tough one."

Sandy hugged her back. "I never appreciated how complicated parenthood could be."

"Welcome to the club," Maggie said. "Not to be a complete downer, but as they get bigger, their problems do, too."

Sandy sighed and glanced at her son with a worried gaze.

Maggie watched Laura playing with Josh, and she realized how similar their childhoods were, except that Laura's father had been a police officer killed in the line of duty when she'd been even younger than Josh. Maggie could only hope that Sandy's husband, Jake, made it home and got to be the father to Josh that her Charlie had never gotten the chance to be to Laura.

When Jake had been deployed, Sandy and Josh had come to live with Maggie. Sandy's own mom, Maggie's sister, had moved to Florida several years ago to take care of their aging mother. It worked out for both of them. Maggie could help with Josh so Sandy could go to school, and it kept the house from being too quiet after Laura had left for college.

"We'll make Christmas special," Maggie said. "No matter what, we'll keep the magic alive for Josh."

"Thanks, Aunt Maggie," she said. "With Mom living in Florida with Nana, I don't know what I'd do without you."

"Speaking of your mom," Maggie said, "when are they planning to arrive?"

"Christmas Eve," Sandy said. "Which is only two weeks away. It's going to be a full house."

"That's all right," Maggie said. "That's what the holidays are all about."

"Well, on that note, if Laura is serious about watching Josh, I'm going to attack my shopping list," Sandy said. She gave Maggie another squeeze and then said good-bye to Laura and Josh.

Laura gave Sandy a five-minute head start before she caved in to Josh's repeated requests to go back to the hammer store. Maggie watched them go. There was something very familiar about seeing Laura and Josh together, and she realized it was almost like watching herself twenty years ago.

The bells on the door rang, and Maggie looked away from the window to greet her customer. The pretty woman who entered was almost unrecognizable. Oh, she still wore glasses and dressed conservatively, but there was a new assertiveness in her stride and a sparkle in her eye that hadn't been there before.

Bianca Madison, presently the richest woman in town, had been sledgehammered by a boatload of tragedy over the past few weeks, but instead of quitting she'd dug in her heels and stood her ground. Maggie was proud of her and was pleased to see that she was holding her own.

"Hi, Bianca," Maggie said. "How are you?"

"I'm doing great," Bianca said.

Bianca beamed at her, and Maggie blinked. Bianca had been through an awful lot over the past few months, not the least of which had been the death of her mother.

"Is there any particular reason?" Maggie asked.

"Yes. In memory of my mother, I've decided to uphold the tradition of the annual open house, but this year it's going to be a holiday ball," Bianca announced. "I'm going to have it the weekend before Christmas, and everyone in town is invited."

Chapter 3

"Are you sure?" Maggie asked. "You've been through an awful lot, and a ball is a huge undertaking. And I'm sure you've noticed it, but the weekend before Christmas is next week."

"Yes, I know. It's perfect. It won't give me a second to be sad. Doc, er, I mean Dad and I talked about it, and he and Max agree that planning a party might keep me from missing my mother so much during the holidays. Besides, I think she would have wanted me to continue the tradition."

Maggie studied the young woman before her. "I think it's an excellent idea. What can I do to help?"

"Stock as many ball gowns as you can," Bianca said. "It's going to be black tie."

"Oh, this is going to be fun," Maggie said.

"Do you think so?" Bianca asked uncertainly.

"Yes, absolutely," she said.

Maggie turned and scanned the area of her shop reserved for formal wear. She had a decent collection started, but she could have used about twice as many gowns.

"I just wish I had more formal wear in house right now. I wasn't planning to load up until prom/wedding season," Maggie said.

"I'm so glad you said that, because I happen to have a truckload of gowns that I hope to donate to your shop," Bianca said. "They were Mother's and Grandmother's and some of my old ones, too. Given that I'm a half foot taller than they were and a few pounds heavier than I used to be, there's just no way I'm ever going to fit into any of them again."

"Are you sure?" Maggie asked.

Bianca nodded.

"I don't think I can take them as a donation," Maggie said. "Why don't we consign them? I mean, your mother's and grandmother's gowns are vintage couture. I'm sure they're worth a fortune. You have to take a percentage of the sales, or I won't be able to carry them in good conscience."

"No," Bianca said. "I want to do this. Consider this a thank-you for all that you've done for me."

"That is very generous, but Bianca, your half sister is still trying to claim the entire estate is hers," Maggie said. She hated to mention it, but she felt she had to. "I don't want to see you penniless."

Bianca smiled at her. "I won't be. I have great faith in my attorney."

"So things are going well with you and Max?" Maggie asked.

Bianca's face turned a charming shade of pink, and Maggie smiled. Max Button, who had been a friend of Maggie's since he'd tutored Laura in high school math, was the local boy genius. Although now that he was in his twenties, he wasn't exactly a boy anymore. Maggie had known that he and Bianca had begun seeing each other. They were the perfect pair, and Maggie was pleased that it seemed to be going so well.

"Still, until the court settles the matter, I insist you take a commission," Maggie said. "I won't feel right about it otherwise."

Bianca gave her a put-upon look that resembled Max at his most exasperated. Maggie laughed.

"Oh, you are spending a lot of time with Max, aren't you?" she asked.

Bianca's blush deepened into a brighter pink. "Is it that obvious?"

"You just made the exact same face he makes when I exasperate him," Maggie said. "Which I do often."

"Max adores you," Bianca said.

"And I him," Maggie said. She put her hand over Bianca's, and said, "I'm glad you two have found each other."

Bianca smiled and nodded. "He's quit delivering pizza, and he's gone to work for Judge Harding."

Maggie raised her eyebrows. "Slacker, ever-student Max has taken a real job?"

Bianca nodded. "And he's got me playing the piano again."

Maggie was so excited she came around the counter and hugged Bianca hard. "This is wonderful. Oh, but what about his art history degree?"

"He's finishing it," she said. "I told him he didn't have to get a real job for me, but he said I gave him a reason to grow up."

Maggie leaned close and whispered, "Do not tell him I said this, but I think I might miss seeing him at the Frosty Freeze in the summer."

"Me, too," Bianca sighed. "But he swears this is what he wants."

She sounded bewildered, and Maggie chuckled. "It sounds like he's in love."

Bianca clapped her hands over her cheeks and her eyes widened behind her glasses. "Do you really think so?"

Maggie nodded, and Bianca dropped her hands from her face and grabbed Maggie's hands in hers. "Oh, I hope you're right, because I am head over heels in love with him. He's just the smartest, funniest, nicest . . ."

"Bianca, are you talking about me again?"

Maggie and Bianca spun to face the door, where Doc Franklin had entered the shop without them noticing.

"Hi, Dad," Bianca said. The name sounded awkward on her tongue, and Maggie figured it was going to take a while for Bianca to get used to having a dad again. "We were just having silly girl talk."

"Well, silly girl, how about our lunch date?" Doc asked.

"Oh, that's right," Bianca said. "I'm sorry, I got caught up talking to Maggie and completely forgot."

"No worries," he said. "Is there any chance you can join us for lunch, Maggie?"

"Thanks, but I brought my own, and I've got to hang around here," she said.

"Okay, how about you come back to work for me, then?" Doc asked.

"If only I could fit four more hours into my days," Maggie said. "I'd be back in a heartbeat."

Maggie had been Doc Franklin's bookkeeper for over twenty years, but after buying her resale store, she'd had to quit working for Doc to give the shop her full attention. Doc was not taking it well and had offered her the old job back every time she'd seen him since.

"Your job will be there if ever you change your mind," he offered.

"Thanks, Doc," Maggie said.

"You're not going to change your mind, are you?"

"No," she said.

He heaved a sigh, but Maggie knew it was more for effect than anything else.

Bianca's phone chimed, and she fished it out of her purse and glanced at the display.

"Oh, it's a text from Tyler Fawkes," she said. "He's agreed to drop off the dresses—if you are willing to take them?"

"On consignment," Maggie said, and Bianca nodded and looked at her dad. "I'll just call him and tell him it's a go, and I'll be ready for lunch."

Doc nodded and watched his daughter step away to make the call with the look of a proud dad. He had only discovered she was his daughter the month before, and although it had caused a major rift in his marriage, he seemed to be making the most of having Bianca in his life.

"You and Bianca seem to be getting on," Maggie said.

"She's a delight," he said. "We have so much in common;

it's really been amazing getting to know her. I wish Alice would . . ."

His voice trailed off, and Maggie patted his hand. Doc had had an affair with Bianca's mother, but he hadn't known that Bianca was his child until Bianca's mother died. Given that his wife, Alice, had been unable to have children, the thing she'd wanted most in life, she took his having a child with someone else as the ultimate betrayal, and she had left him.

Maggie couldn't blame Alice, and neither could Doc, but it was clear to Maggie that Doc still loved his wife, and he struggled with losing her.

"Give her time," Maggie said.

"I don't suppose I have any choice," he said.

Doc forced a smile as Bianca rejoined them.

"It's all set," Bianca said. "Tyler will deliver the dresses today, which is perfect, as the invitations will go out tomorrow."

"I can't wait to do my window display," Maggie said. "This is going to be the best holiday ball ever."

Invitations were not necessary, as word of Bianca Madison's ball began to spread through St. Stanley with the roar of a wildfire.

Maggie and Tyler had just finished unloading his truck into her storage area at the back of the shop when Joanne arrived to ask Maggie if she'd heard.

Maggie waved good-bye to Tyler and closed and locked the door behind him. It had been a long day, and she was ready to go home and snuggle Josh while they shared some hot chocolate and cookies.

Joanne's eyes were huge as she took in Maggie's storage room. "Bianca gave you all of these to sell?"

"Yep," Maggie said. "I'm selling them on a consignment basis."

Joanne fingered a gorgeous chocolate velvet gown with an empire waist and cap sleeves. With her long, dark hair, she'd look like a heroine right out of a Jane Austen novel if she wore the gown.

"Do you want me to put that one aside for you?" Maggie asked. "I'm going to be doing inventory tomorrow."

Joanne took it off of its rack and held it up to her front. She glanced up at Maggie, and her face crumpled.

"Don't bother," she wailed. "I'm too fat for it."

Maggie's eyes went wide. "Oh, honey, don't be silly. You're not too fat. You're just pregnant."

"I'm fat," Joanne sobbed. "I can't zip my pants anymore, and my boobs are huge."

Maggie looked from the dress to Joanne. The empire cut would absolutely work over her belly, and the bustline was going to be very voluptuous, but totally doable.

"I think the huge-boob thing is good with this dress," Maggie said. "Just think—Michael won't be able to take his eyes off you."

"Huh," Joanne scoffed.

"What was that about?" Maggie asked. She knew Joanne was hormonal, but honestly, this was like a roller coaster without safety bars.

"Michael hired a new girl at the deli. She's young and gorgeous and not fat." Joanne's voice ended on a wail that rolled into a flurry of sobs.

Maggie looked at her friend and then handed her a tissue from the box on the counter. "Is that what this is all about? Are you jealous of some woman Michael has hired?"

"No . . . yes," Joanne admitted, still sobbing.

"Oh, come here, honey," Maggie said. She opened her arms, and Joanne walked into her hug, still clutching the brown velvet to her chest. Maggie stroked her back and made soothing noises until Joanne's snuffles subsided.

"Better now?" Maggie asked.

"A little."

"Joanne, what you're feeling is perfectly normal," Maggie said. "Every woman gets a little turfy over her man when she's pregnant."

"They do?"

Maggie stepped back and carefully took the dress out of Joanne's hands before it was crushed beyond saving. As she hung it up, she remembered being pregnant with Laura, and she laughed.

"Yes, in fact, I made Ginger ride shotgun with me one night when I tailed Charlie in his squad car, just because I thought he was spending too much time at the diner eating pie. There was a cute waitress who worked there back then, and I was sure she was planning to put her hooks into my man."

"And did she?" Joanne asked.

"No," Maggie said with a shake of her head. "She was studying to be a teacher and in fact is now the principal of the middle school."

"Rosie Donahue?" Joanne asked.

"She was Rosie Gilbert back then," Maggie said. "You should have seen Charlie's and Roger's faces when they found Ginger and me asleep in our car at the diner."

"Asleep?"

"We parked and waited for him to come out of the diner so we could tail him, but we fell asleep. Ginger was pregnant with her oldest boy, Aaron, at the time. Well, when Roger and Charlie couldn't find us, they about went crazy, and then someone spotted our car and called Roger. Well, needless to say, we woke up to find two very unhappy husbands."

"So Charlie wasn't interested in the waitress?" Joanne asked.

"Not even a little," Maggie said. "And you know Michael isn't interested in this new employee either."

"I know," Joanne said. She sounded like she meant it, yet Maggie could hear the *but* in her voice.

"But?" she asked.

"Usually, Michael talks to me about who he is going to hire," Joanne said. She fretted her lower lip. "I didn't even know he wanted more help, and he never said a word about Diane. Diane Jenkins is her name, and she is annoyingly pretty and single, and he seems awfully attentive of her."

"Of course he didn't mention her," Maggie said. "He knows how tired you are with the baby. The last thing he wants to do is burden you with silly business stuff that he can handle on his own. He probably hired her so that when the baby comes he can be around more."

"You think so?" Joanne asked.

"I know it," Maggie said. "Just like we get turfy, they get very protective. It's really very sweet. So let him shoulder the burden for a while, and you just take care of you and that baby."

Joanne beamed at her. "I never thought of it that way. I bet you're right. You'll hold the dress for me?"

"Of course," Maggie said. Joanne gave her a quick hug, and Maggie let her out the front door and locked it behind her.

She heaved a sigh of relief that disaster had been averted, but she also made a mental note to go check out this Diane Jenkins at the first possible opportunity.

It certainly wouldn't hurt for the young woman to meet the rest of the Good Buy Girls and know that Joanne traveled in a very protective pack.

Chapter 4

"So, who are you going to the ball with?" Laura asked Maggie the next day as they arranged one of the dresses Bianca had dropped off in the front window.

"You," Maggie said. "Unless you have other plans."

"Oh, come on. You know Pete Daniels is going to ask you," she said. "He seems awfully nice, and he always has a joke at the ready."

"He is a very nice man," Maggie agreed.

"But?"

"No buts," Maggie said.

"Really?" Laura asked. Her look was sly, and Maggie frowned. "What about Sam Collins? Word on the street is that he's got a thing for you."

"Would that street be Inaccurate Road?" Maggie asked.

"Ha-ha-ha," Laura said, but she smiled. "He's got really nice blue eyes."

Maggie's head snapped up. "When did you see Sam's eyes?"

"Well, they were walking down the street . . ."

"Ha-ha-ha back at you," Maggie said.

"He was in the Daily Grind," Laura said. "He and Pete were joking about which one of them should ask you to the ball. They asked me what I thought, and I told them a nice two out of three on rock, paper, scissors should do it."

"You didn't!"

"Okay, I didn't," Laura said. Maggie could tell by the twinkle in her eye, however, that she had.

"That does it," Maggie said. "I'm not going."

"Oh no, you have to go," Laura said. "It won't be any fun without you."

And just like that, Maggie knew she'd be going. How often did she and Laura get to dress up and go to a party together? She wasn't going to miss this chance because Pete and Sam were morons. In fact, having Laura here was the perfect excuse to say no to the both of them.

"Fine, but you're my date," she said.

"Only if you're mine," Laura agreed. "No throwing each other over for the first handsome face that comes along either."

"Agreed," Maggie said.

"Good." Laura glanced out the window. "Because handsome number one is on the move."

"What?" Maggie dropped the dress she was draping on a mannequin. "Where? Which one? How do I look?"

"Oh yeah, not going to throw me over, huh?" Laura laughed. "It's Pete. Oh, he's met up with Claire. Now they're walking together. Yep, they are definitely coming this way."

Maggie blew out a breath of relief. She liked Pete, she really did, but he did not make her as nervous as Sam did, which was undoubtedly why she felt relieved that it was Pete and not Sam. The bells on the door chimed, and Pete strode in with Claire beside him.

Hellos were exchanged all around, and Maggie was pleased with the praise, even if it was over the top, from Pete and Claire over her window display.

"So, if rock beats scissors, and scissors beats paper, and paper beats rock, what beats all three of them?" Pete asked with a conspiratorial wink at Laura, who grinned at him

Maggie and Claire exchanged a look, and then they shook their heads at Pete.

"Chuck Norris," he said.

Maggie and Laura chuckled, but Claire busted up, slapping Pete on the shoulder. He gave her a bright smile, and it struck Maggie that Pete and Claire would make a perfect couple. She was mid-thirties, he was early forties. They were both book lovers and, best of all, Pete made her laugh, which Claire sorely needed, given the dark days of her past.

"So, Pete, do you have a date for the ball?" Maggie asked.

"Uh, no," he said. "I haven't asked anyone yet. Why?"

He seemed so hopeful that Maggie felt bad, until she glanced at Claire, who looked rueful, as if she figured Maggie was about to ask Pete and there went her chance.

"Well, you need to get on that," Maggie said. "Not to brag or anything, but I have three dates."

"Three?" Pete asked, looking surprised.

"Yes, my daughter, my niece, and my grand-nephew and I are all going together. No pretty boys allowed," Maggie said.

She was pleased that her voice sounded casual and not as if she and Laura had cooked this up so she could avoid going with Pete.

"We figured we'd never get another chance to do it up together, so we wanted to enjoy this one. Besides, with Sandy's husband still stationed in Afghanistan, I think this might be hard for her."

She saw Laura shrug at Pete out of the corner of her eye as if this was news to her, and he nodded. He looked accepting while Claire looked hopeful. Maggie wanted to toss a shoe at Pete's head. A really great date was standing right next to him, the big doofus, and he didn't even notice.

In the end, it was Laura who connected the dots for him.

"So, Claire, what about you? Hot date, or do you want to join us?"

"Oh, I wouldn't want to intrude on a family thing," she said. "I don't know that I'll be going. I'm not really comfortable in crowds."

Pete turned to look at her, and their eyes met. Maggie held her breath. How could he not notice the cute, curvy librarian with the bobbed blonde hair and smart-girl glasses? *Come on!* she wanted to yell, but she didn't.

"Well, if you're looking for someone to buffer you from the crowd, I'd be happy to take you to the ball," Pete said. His voice sounded strained, and Maggie thought his cheeks had the faintest tinge of pink. Was he nervous asking Claire? She took that as a very promising sign.

"I . . . uh . . . I would like that," Claire stammered. Maggie almost fell out of the window from relief.

"Excellent. It's a date," he said. They grinned at each

other, and he left the shop whistling. He didn't even remember to wave good-bye to Maggie or Laura as he went.

"Oh my god," Claire said as she slumped onto a nearby poufy chair. "I have a date!"

"Yes, you do," Maggie said. "So, what are you going to wear?"

"Oh, I don't know," Claire said. "I haven't had to dress for anything formal since I can't even remember when."

"Well, isn't it fortunate that I have a plethora of dresses for you to choose from?" Maggie asked.

Claire looked delighted, and then her face fell.

"You know Pete came here to ask you to go to the ball," she said. "Don't you?"

"I have no such information," Maggie said. "As far as I'm concerned, it worked out exactly as it was supposed to."

"Are you sure?" Claire asked. "If you like him, I would totally understand and cancel the date. I mean, he's cute and funny, and he likes you. Everyone knows that."

"But he didn't ask me, he asked you," Maggie said. She looked Claire right in the eyes so that Claire knew she was being straight with her. "I do like Pete, but just as a friend."

"Oh, good." Claire sagged. "Because I really like him, but you know the rule. . . ."

"Sisters before misters," the three of them said together and then shared a smile.

"Mom, what about that deep blue chiffon number with the silver halter straps?" Laura asked. "Claire would totally rock that dress. Pete won't even know what hit him."

"Oh, and I have some silver sandals," Claire said.

"Perfect," Maggie said. "Go try it on, and if it needs

alterations, you can take it to Mrs. Kellerman at the dry cleaner. She has serious needle skills."

Laura led Claire off in search of the dress while Maggie went to check out her window display from the outside. She had gone with a winter-wonderland theme. She had draped the window in dark blue velvet and had shimmering white snowflakes suspended on different lengths of fishing wire hanging all around her mannequins.

She stood on the sidewalk, examining her window from every angle. She had to admit it looked festive and fun with a handsome couple all dressed up in a tuxedo and ball gown with glittery snowflakes falling all around them. Laura's gold box accented the window perfectly with the sign for free gift wrap facing the door as people walked into the shop.

"Excuse me." A voice interrupted her scrutiny. "Is the gown in the window for sale?"

Maggie turned to see a handsome, dark-haired man in a camel overcoat standing beside her.

"Excuse me?" she asked, sure she must have heard him wrong.

"Is this your shop?"

"Yes," she said.

"I was wondering if that gown is for sale," he said.

Maggie glanced at the Anne Barge gown. Simple white satin with a black-and-white floral embroidered hem and a long black satin ribbon that was tied in a bow at the waist and embellished with a glittery brooch, the gown was a work of art and by far her favorite of all the gowns Bianca had dropped off. Maggie was all about resale, but somehow she knew that selling this gown was going to hurt.

"Yes, it is." She forced the words out.

"Excellent," he said. He looked so pleased that Maggie had a hard time begrudging him the dress. "I want to buy it for my soon-to-be wife. I think she'll love it. Is it by any chance a size six?"

"Yes, it is," Maggie said. That settled it. How could she feel bad about the sale when it was such a romantic gesture and it was the perfect size?

"If you'd like, we do gift wrap free of charge," she said as she led the way into the store.

"That'd be nice," he said. "I'm sure you'll do a much better job than I would, given my ham-fisted tendency with tape and scissors."

"Are you and your fiancée going to the Madison ball?" Maggie asked. "It's going to be the event of the season in St. Stanley."

The man smiled. "It should be a wonderful time."

"Oh, I'm Maggie Gerber, by the way," she said and held out her hand.

"Blake," he said as he took her hand in his. "Blake Caulfield."

"So, you're a friend of Bianca Madison's?" she asked.

"My fiancée is an acquaintance of hers," he said. "I haven't met her yet."

"Oh, she's delightful. You'll like her," Maggie said as she climbed back up into the window and carefully stripped the mannequin.

"I'm looking forward to it," he said. Maggie handed the dress down to him and climbed out of the window.

"Have you been engaged for long?" she asked.

"Not as long as I'd like," he said with a grin. "The fact

is, she gave me a heck of a chase, but I finally made her mine."

Maggie took the dress back from him and headed over to the wrapping table.

"Well," she said, "she's a lucky woman to have such a thoughtful fiancé."

"Oh, wow. You sold the Barge gown," Laura said as she joined them.

Maggie glanced at Laura and knew her daughter was feeling the same mix of emotions that she had felt at the thought of selling it.

"Do you want to take over the wrapping while I ring it up?" she asked.

Laura nodded. "Would you prefer gold or silver paper, Mr. . . ."

"Caulfield," Maggie said. "Blake Caulfield, this is my daughter, Laura Gerber."

"How do you do?" Blake gave her a warm smile as they shook hands. "Please call me Blake."

"All right, Blake. Which do you prefer?" Laura asked as she held up the two papers.

He looked perplexed, and asked, "Which do you think?"

"Well, I like the silver with a navy blue velvet ribbon," Laura said. "Very elegant."

Blake tipped his head as he considered it. "Elegant. I think that would be perfect for my girl. Thank you."

Laura smiled and set to the wrapping while Maggie led the way to the cash register. Blake took out his wallet, and Maggie was surprised when he counted out five crisp one-hundred-dollar bills.

He caught her look and grinned. "I hadn't planned on

dropping all of my Christmas shopping budget in one store on one item, but . . ."

He shrugged, and Maggie smiled.

"If it makes you feel better, this is an amazing bargain," she said. "You're getting seventy-five-percent off."

"It does," he said. "Thanks."

When Maggie had done the inventory for the gowns, she'd discovered that the Barge gown retailed at over two thousand dollars, but on consignment it was a smokin' hot deal for less than five hundred.

Most of the residents in the small town of St. Stanley didn't have that kind of money to spend, which was why Maggie had figured the gown would be in the front window for a while. But Blake Caulfield wasn't a local, and he didn't look like money was a big issue. His camel overcoat was cashmere, his watch was gold and his loafers had a newly polished sheen to them.

She glanced at the wallet he'd left open on the counter. A photo of a pretty brunette girl standing on the beach with the wind tossing her hair across her face was visible in the picture holder.

"Is that your fiancée?" Maggie asked. Blake nodded and held the picture up for her to see more clearly.

"Yes, that's Ann," he said.

"She's lovely," Maggie said. "That dress is going to be stunning on her."

Blake gave her a charming grin. "I think so, too."

Maggie counted out his change and handed it back to him with the receipt. "If for some reason it doesn't fit, you can always bring it back."

"Thanks," he said.

"Okay, what do you think?" Claire asked as she stepped out of the dressing room.

Maggie felt her mouth slide open in surprise. Claire looked gorgeous. The blue brought out her eyes and complimented her pale skin tone. The halter cut to the bodice made her figure go va-va-va-voom while the straight line of the skirt flirted around her legs, making them seem longer than they were.

"Pete is going to have a heart attack," she said.

"Do you think so?" Claire asked, looking pleased.

"Definitely," Blake said, and he put his hand over his chest as if to check to see if he was having one.

Claire laughed in delight and then looked down. "It's about three inches too long for me, but that's easy to fix, right?"

"It'll be a snap for Mrs. Kellerman," Maggie said. "Why don't you walk over there with it on, so she can pin it?"

"But I need to pay you," Claire protested.

"Please," Maggie said, and waved a hand at her. "I know where you live. You can pay me later."

Claire grinned and hurried back to the dressing room to slip on her loafers and grab her coat for the short walk next door.

Laura brought the large, beautifully wrapped box over to the counter.

"Well, that's almost too pretty to open," Blake said as he hefted the box in his arms. "Almost."

"Thank you," Laura beamed. "I hope she loves it as much as we do."

"She will," he assured them. "Thank you, lovely ladies."

On the way out, he passed Summer Phillips, who had

just yanked open the door. She scowled at him as he walked by her, and he gave Maggie an alarmed look and hurried out the door.

"Summer, I think you need to back up and try that entrance again," Maggie snapped. "I will not have you frightening off my customers."

"As if I care what you think," Summer said.

She was wearing patent-leather thigh-high boots with spike heels and a red velvet halter with a matching cropped jacket and a miniskirt with gold jingle bells sewn onto the hem. It was the same outfit she'd worn for her tawdry window display photo, and Maggie wondered if this was going to be her uniform of choice for the rest of the month.

"What do you want, Summer?" she asked.

"You mean other than to impale you on the heel of my shoe?" she asked.

Maggie rolled her right hand at her to indicate that Summer should hurry up with whatever her issue was, as she was running out of patience.

"I know all about the Madison ball," Summer said. "And I know that Bianca gave you a bunch of moldy old dresses to sell. But you're not going to get away with it, because I'm going to tell Courtney. Bianca can't sell off property that belongs equally to her half sister."

"I fail to see what this has to do with me," Maggie said. "And I certainly don't see what it has to do with you. So, if that's all . . ."

Maggie came around the sales counter and started walking toward Summer. She must have had fire in her eyes, because Summer began to back up as Maggie marched toward her.

Laura, as if sensing where this was going, hurried to the front door and pushed it open.

"I'm going to get the sheriff over here, and he'll see to it that you give back every single one of those dresses," Summer blustered.

"Whatever." Maggie shrugged and kept walking. "Are we done now? Because I really have so many more important things to do."

Summer stopped walking. She was so mad she was practically vibrating in place.

"Oh, you think you're so special," Summer seethed. "Just because Bianca invited you to her ball. Well, you're not."

Maggie paused. She noticed for the first time that it was more than rage behind Summer's upset. There was also a little bit of hurt.

"Summer, were you not invited to the ball?" she asked.

"No, I—" Summer's voice broke and she glared at Maggie. "It's none of your business, and speaking of your business, your days are numbered. Second Time Around is going to squash you this holiday season. Consider yourself warned."

"Oh, for goodness's sake," Maggie said. "Get out, and take your ridiculous outfit and all of your junior high drama with you. I am so over this. Step one toe into my shop again, and I'll see that it's the last step you take."

She charged, and Summer backed right out the door, which Laura yanked shut after her.

Laura gave Maggie a wide-eyed look, and Maggie laughed. It was a stress-busting gust of laughter and Laura gave her a surprised look before she started laughing, too.

Like all good giggle fits, it didn't end until tears came out of their eyes and their bellies had cramped.

"Did you see her face?" Laura asked as she wiped her cheeks with her sleeves.

"Priceless," Maggie said with a sigh.

"What did I miss?" Claire asked as she came out of the dressing room and glanced between them.

For no particular reason the confused expression on Claire's face set Maggie off again, which set Laura off, too, and then Claire started laughing, because the giggles are contagious. Naturally, it was in this semi-hysterical state that Sam Collins walked in.

"Would anyone care to tell me why Summer says you threatened to kill her?" he asked.

Chapter 5

Maggie howled at Sam's question, but Laura looked outraged.

"That's ridiculous!" Laura said. "All she did was strongly suggest that Summer stay out of the shop."

"How strongly?" Sam asked.

"Strong like Superwoman," Maggie said. Her face was flushed with laughter, and she pumped her fist.

"Did you clobber her?" Sam asked in alarm.

Maggie was sobered by the horrified look on his face, and she sighed.

"No, I was merely very firm. I really have had it with her, Sam. I've tried to be nice, but enough is enough. She comes into my shop all the time. I never go into hers. If she would stay out of mine, we'd really never see each other."

Sam nodded. His blue eyes sparkled at her, and he said, "But wouldn't you miss her?"

"Not even a little," Maggie said with a frown.

"Hey, Laura, come keep me company over at the dry cleaner, would you?" Claire asked. "If there's a line, I'm going to feel like an idiot wearing this dress."

"All right," Laura agreed. "Back in a sec, Mom."

Maggie watched as the two exited the shop, and she was left alone with Sam. Had Claire done that on purpose? Maggie shook her head. Claire was the most straightforward person she'd ever met. If she were planning to set Maggie up, she'd be much less subtle about it.

Maggie glanced at Sam. Although he stopped by every now and again, she hadn't seen much of him over the past few weeks. Getting her shop up and running had taken all of her time and energy.

"The shop looks good," he said as he glanced around the room. "How're you settling in here?"

"Thanks," Maggie said. "I'm doing all right. I think it's going well, but given that I've never owned a business before, that could just be naïve optimism speaking."

She tucked a stray strand of auburn hair behind her ear and glanced around her store. It had turned out well, and business had been decent. If the sale of the Barge dress this morning was any indicator, she was going to have a very merry holiday season indeed.

"So, are you going to Bianca's swank ball?" Sam asked.

Maggie turned to face him. His blue eyes locked on hers, and she felt a sudden flutter of nerves hit her low and deep. What would she do if Sam asked her? Was he here to ask her? She'd already agreed to a girls-only evening.

"I'm going with Sandy and Laura," she said. "Since Jake is still in Afghanistan, we didn't want Sandy to feel left out."

Sam gave her a warm smile. "So no hot date with Pete Daniels, then?"

"No. In fact, he's taking Claire," she said.

Sam raised his eyebrows. "Well, that is good news."

"How do you mean?" she asked.

"I like Claire," he said. "It'd be nice to see her with a good guy like Pete. He's got a great sense of humor, and he makes a righteous cup of coffee."

"Agreed," Maggie said.

Claire's last known boyfriend had been a murderer who had been murdered himself. During Sam's first month as sheriff, he'd had to take Claire into custody, as she had been the most likely suspect. It had gotten Maggie and Sam's new friendship off to a rocky start.

The bells on the door chimed as a group of three women came in. Maggie greeted them with a smile, and Sam turned to leave.

Abruptly, he turned back to the counter and leaned over it. His mouth was just inches from Maggie's ear, and he whispered in a voice only Maggie could hear, "Oh, and I really like that my competition is giving up and going after someone else."

Maggie stared after him as he crossed the room to the door. He pushed the door open and stepped out and then turned and winked at Maggie as the door shut behind him. She felt her jaw slide open in surprise. Did he mean . . . ?

"Maggie, you have to help me," Sydney Lewis said. "Phil has asked me to the Madison ball, and I need a dress. It has to be an amazing gown, something that will make his eyes pop out of his head and a proposal fall from his lips."

It took all of Maggie's power of concentration to drag her

attention away from the door and study Sydney. She looked the young woman over. With her black hair, olive skin and dark brown eyes, there was really only one choice. "How do you feel about the color red?"

"Orange-toned red or purple-toned red?" Sydney asked.

"Purple red, definitely," Maggie said.

"Show me," Sydney said with a grin.

The day passed in a blur of dress fittings and referrals to the dry cleaner for tailoring, as people started gearing up for the ball. Maggie loved hearing the sound of the receipt printer as she rang up each sale.

By the time she and Laura lowered the blinds and locked up the store, she was weary all the way to her bones. The thought of being curled up in bed with a good book called to her like a siren song, but she knew she had one more errand to run before her day was done.

With her mother and sister coming up from Florida, she was hosting the holiday feast, and she needed to order her holiday ham. She and Laura made their way over to More than Meats, Joanne and Michael's deli.

She knew they were keeping extended hours due to the holiday season, and Maggie and Laura got to the store just before it closed.

Stewart Paulson was leaving with a deli platter, so Laura held the door open to let him pass before they entered.

"Well, if it isn't my favorite ladies of resale," Michael called from behind the counter.

He grinned at them, and Maggie smiled back. She had always liked Joanne's husband, Michael. With his overabundance of enthusiasm and good cheer, he reminded her of a big kid. Michael had the gift of being able to make his customers feel happier than when they'd come in. Maggie admired this smart business trait and tried to emulate it in her own shop.

"Hi, Michael," she said. "I'm so glad we made it before you closed. I need to order my holiday ham."

"Sure thing," he said. "Are we going with the honey-baked?"

"Absolutely," Maggie said. "I need one big enough to feed a family of five women and one boy."

"I think I can manage that," Michael said.

A petite blonde came through the swinging door behind him, hefting a tray almost as big as she was. She maneuvered it into the display case and straightened up. She glanced over the counter at Maggie and Laura and gave them a shy smile. Maggie didn't recognize her, and assumed she must be the reason for Joanne's jealous meltdown.

"Diane, I want you to meet some friends of mine and Joanne's," he said.

Maggie took it as an excellent sign that Michael mentioned Joanne in that statement. If he had a thing for Diane, wouldn't he try to avoid mentioning his pregnant wife?

"Nice to meet you," the young woman said.

Diane glanced over at them, but she kept her eyes downcast, as if she was nervous to make eye contact. Maggie wondered if it was more than shyness that made her so aloof. Maybe it was a guilty conscience. Maybe Joanne's radar wasn't that far off, and the cute young blonde had a thing for Michael, and Joanne had sensed it.

"You, too," Maggie said.

"Are you new to St. Stanley?" Laura asked. Her voice was kind, and Maggie was proud to see her daughter reaching out to the young woman, even though she wasn't yet sure Diane was the sort of girl Laura should befriend.

"Yes," Diane answered, but her eyes darted around the room as if she was looking for someone.

"Where are you from?" Laura asked.

Diane sent Michael a nervous look, but he nodded at her as if to let her know that it was okay.

"I'm from up north," Diane said.

"I go to school in Pennsylvania," Laura said. "I'm on break now for the holidays. You know, I never realized how quiet St. Stanley is until I went away."

Diane gave her a small smile. "I like it here. It feels safe."

"Well, if you ever want to catch a movie—" Laura offered, but Diane interrupted her.

"Thanks, but I'd better get back," she said. "We have lots of special orders."

Diane turned and pushed through the doors and disappeared back into the kitchen.

Maggie looked at Michael. "Well, she seems nice."

He looked after his employee with a sad smile. "She is," he said. "She just needs time. She's been through some rough stuff."

"Oh, well, make sure you bring her to the Madison ball," Maggie said. "It'll give her a chance to meet people."

"I'll try and talk her into it," he said. "She's pretty shy, though. That sort of thing may be too much for her."

"I'll stop by tomorrow and invite her for coffee," Laura said. "Moving can be a lonely transition. Maybe I can help her with it."

"That'd be nice, Laura," Michael said. "Usually, Joanne

spends more time with the new staff, but I know she's caught up with the baby . . ."

He frowned, and Maggie suspected he knew it was more than the baby. She wanted to tell him what Joanne was going through, but she didn't want to betray her friend's confidence.

"You know, a pregnant woman has a lot of hormones rocketing through her," Maggie said. "Sometimes they just don't make sense."

Michael met her concerned gaze with a hopeful one, "Really? It's normal?"

"Perfectly," Maggie assured him. "Just be attentive and she'll be all right."

"Would flowers be a good move?" he asked.

"Flowers are always a good move," Maggie said.

Michael grinned. "I can do that."

Maggie and Laura left the deli, and Maggie felt relieved. Yes, Diane was pretty, but Michael showed no sign of being interested in her. If anything, he seemed big-brotherly toward her, like he was looking out for her. And he was obviously worried about Joanne.

As they walked back to the shop, where Maggie's car was parked, Laura slipped her arm through her mother's, and said, "You know, Claire and I were betting that Sam Collins stopped by the shop to ask you to the ball. So, did he?"

"Nope."

"Really? We were so sure. I mean, it's so obvious that he likes you. You know that, right?"

"I know no such thing," Maggie said.

She felt her cheeks grow warm, and she was grateful that the winter night was dark, so she could hide her face.

"Aw, come on. The man obviously likes you," Laura said. "He looks at you like you're a chicken and he's a chicken hawk."

"A chicken?" Maggie asked. "That's the best analogy you can come up with? How exactly did you get into that fancy-pants college of yours?"

"You're a really pretty chicken," Laura teased.

"Yeah, because Butterballs are known for that," Maggie said. "I can't tell you what this conversation is doing for my self-esteem."

"I thought Butterballs were turkeys," Laura said.

They reached Maggie's car, and she unlocked the doors with the button on her key chain. Mercifully, the poultry talk seemed to have gotten Laura off track, for which Maggie was grateful. She did not want to discuss Sam Collins.

As they climbed in, Laura turned and studied Maggie under the dome light.

"Dad would want you to be happy," she said.

"I am happy."

"Mom," Laura groaned. "You know what I mean. I think dad would approve of Sam. And, you know, everyone agrees that Sam and you would be really good together."

"Define *everyone*," Maggie said.

"Claire, Ginger, Joanne, Michael, Bianca, Max—"

"Okay, okay, I get it," Maggie said. "You all are a bunch of gossips."

"No, we all just want to see you happy," Laura countered. Maggie started to protest again that she was happy, but

Laura held up her hand. "Just think about what I said. Please."

Maggie nodded, but only to end the conversation. She had no intention of thinking about being happy with Sam Collins. Period.

Yes, he had called Pete his competition and had said he was glad that Pete was taking Claire to the ball, but what did that mean exactly? She couldn't tell, probably because every time she saw him, her brain turned to goo. Except when he smiled at her, and that was even worse.

"Mom?" Laura's voice broke into her thoughts.

"Yes?"

"The keys go in the ignition," she said with a laugh. "Maybe you should wait to think over what I said until after we get home."

Maggie glanced at Laura and saw her laughing. With a half-hearted annoyed huff, she put the keys in and started the car. When exactly had her daughter gotten too smart for her own good?

Chapter 6

The next week was a flurry of business for Maggie, as everyone was gearing up for the ball. The bells on her door seemed to chime repeatedly, and the *cha-ching* of the cash register made a very festive accompaniment.

It was the day before the ball when Laura showed up for her shift with Diane from the deli in tow. The petite blonde looked edgy around the crowd of women, all trying on gowns, but Laura stayed by her side, and Maggie noticed that Diane relaxed enough to joke around with Laura.

"I can't wear that," Diane said with a grin as Laura held up an enormous sparkly yellow dress with a huge poofy skirt in front of her. "I'd look like a gumdrop."

"It's true!" Laura cried. "I'll wear a matching orange one, and we can go as the Gumdrop Girls."

As the two busted up with laughter, Maggie shook her head. Laura had spent a lot of time over the past week befriending Diane. Maggie had gotten to know her a little better and had revised her opinion. She didn't think Diane was after Michael but rather that she looked up to him as a father figure. Laura hadn't given her the specifics, but Maggie sensed from what Laura did say that Diane was going through a difficult time.

Out of the corner of her eye, she caught a glimpse of lavender. It was a simple Elie Saab couture gown with a fitted top and lacy floor-length skirt. Diane would look amazing in it. Maggie took it off the rack and approached the two girls, who were still laughing, and held it up in front of Diane.

"Despite the allure of a gumdrop, this one might suit you better," she said.

Diane took the dress and turned to see what it would look like in the mirror behind her. It made her light blue eyes reflect the lavender and complemented her skin tone. She sighed as she fingered the fabric.

"It's lovely, but I could never afford to buy a dress like this," she said. She went to hand it back to Maggie.

"So rent it from us," Maggie said with a shrug.

"Rent it?" she asked.

"Yes, I've wanted to try renting out gowns and things that people do not need to wear more than once," Maggie said. "You can be my test case."

Laura clapped her hands and hugged her new friend.

"It's the perfect solution. Thanks, Mom."

"Oh, I don't know," Diane said. "Honestly, I'm not sure that a big holiday ball is really my thing."

"Oh no," Laura said. "You have to come. Everyone in town is going to be there, and it'll be so much better than sitting at home alone."

Diane's eyes got wide when Laura said the word *alone*, and Maggie could swear she saw a flicker of fear.

"Are you all right?" she asked Diane but was interrupted when Britney Bergstrom stormed over to them.

"That one!" Britney pointed her finger at the gown still in Diane's hands. "I have to have that one."

"Sorry," Maggie said, "but Diane has already chosen it."

Maggie didn't much care for Britney Bergstrom. She had been one year ahead of Laura in school, and she had been one of the mean girls. She was the daughter of overly indulgent parents and as such had grown up with an unhealthy level of entitlement. What Britney wanted Britney got, but not today.

"Excuse me?" Britney blinked at the three of them as if they had begun speaking a language she didn't understand. "I said I want it."

"Yes, and I'm sorry," Maggie said. "But Diane is taking that one. If it's the color you're partial to, I'm sure I have another—"

"I don't think you heard me." Britney stomped one platform high heel on the floor. Her tone was shrill as she raised her voice and said, "I. Want. That. One."

The entire shop went still as everyone turned to watch the scene unfolding before them. Maggie could see several of the older women in the room staring at Britney in disapproval while a few of the younger ones looked on in awe. Maggie knew that this altercation was going to cost her a customer, but given that she didn't really like this particular customer, she was okay with that.

"I'm sorry, but you'll need to pick something else," Maggie said. She was pleased that her voice remained even.

Britney's face went red, and Maggie was pretty sure smoke was going to start billowing out of her ears.

"She can have it, really," Diane said. "I don't want to cause any problems." Her voice sounded submissive and Maggie felt a flicker of annoyance with the young woman.

"See?" Britney asked in triumph. She reached out to snatch the gown from Diane, but Laura stepped in between them.

"No, I don't see," Laura said. "You've been told to pick something else. Do so or leave."

Laura's gaze flickered to her mother and Maggie gave her a small nod.

"How dare you?" Britney huffed.

Laura rolled her eyes. "Really? That's the best you've got? Why don't you just trot your underdressed booty over to Dumontville and hit the Neiman Marcus or Nordstrom? I mean, isn't it beneath you to buy resale?"

"Nice try," Britney said. "But everyone knows vintage couture is hot, and the Madison family has the best collection of couture clothing in Virginia. Now you either give me that dress, or I swear I'll ruin you."

Maggie stared at her. She hadn't handled unhappy patients and unhappy insurance-company reps for twenty years for nothing. She knew customer service was critical for her business, but it was *her* business, and she wasn't about to allow anyone to bully her or her other customers. Period.

She looked Britney up and down, and in her calmest voice said, "Get out."

Britney gasped. The crowd of shoppers parted as if making way for Britney to leave. Maggie stepped forward. Britney stepped back. This continued all the way to the door, which someone was kind enough to push open.

Britney had bright red spots of embarrassment flaming her cheeks as she glanced over Maggie's head to glare at Diane. Like any bully, she was going for the weak one.

"You're going to pay for this," she said.

"Oh, please," Maggie snapped. "Enough with the drama. Why don't you go across the street and shop with your own kind?"

She yanked the door shut, leaving Britney Bergstrom standing outside gaping at her.

The crowd in the room burst into a ripple of murmurs and a smattering of applause and resumed shopping, but Maggie's gaze was on Diane, who looked visibly shaken.

"Are you all right?" Laura asked Diane as Maggie rejoined them.

Diane gave her a wan smile. "I'm afraid I'm not very good at confrontation."

"I'm sorry that was stressful," Maggie said. "But you can't let people like Britney push you around."

Diane gave her a nod, but it was timid, as if she really didn't believe what Maggie was saying.

"Come on," Laura said. "Let's go try on that dress and then you'll feel better."

Diane glanced down at the dress in her arms. "It really is beautiful." She glanced up at Maggie, and her eyes were damp with unshed tears. "Thank you."

"You're welcome."

Maggie smiled at Diane before turning back to the line of customers she had waiting at the counter. A little part of her, the bad part, couldn't help but glance out the window to see Britney cross the street to Summer's shop. As far as she was concerned, the two of them deserved each other.

"Well, that was quite a show," a voice said from behind her. Maggie knew without looking that it was Ginger.

"Meh. I can live with that," Maggie said as she turned around with a grin for her friend. "I never could stand Britney or her mother when we were on the PTO together."

"Ugh. Remember the time they wanted us all to wear matching rhinestone-studded shirts while waving pompoms to march in the Memorial Day parade as PTO moms?"

"Horrifying," Maggie agreed with a shudder. "So, what did you find?"

Ginger had an amazing figure for a woman who had birthed four strapping young lads, and she'd chosen the perfect dress to showcase it. A black sequined curve-hugger that was going to leave Roger a slobbering mess.

"Oh, nice," Maggie said.

"Thanks," Ginger said. "Is that Diane Jenkins with Laura? Is she the one Joanne was so jealous of?"

"Yes," Maggie said. "But I think it was just hormones on Joanne's part. Diane and Laura have become friends, and Diane seems awfully nice."

"Well good," Ginger said. "I did not want to have to go slap Michael upside the head."

"Awkward," Maggie agreed.

"So, has Sam been by?" Ginger asked. Her look was sly, and Maggie shook her head.

"He did not ask me to the ball," Maggie said, "if you're fishing."

"Of course I am," she said. "But I already know that.

Sam told Roger that you said you were going with Laura and Sandy and that was it."

"I can't believe your husband and Sam have such candid conversations. I didn't think they strayed beyond football scores and baseball stats."

"Roger knows better than to come home after beers with Sam without any information. He does not like sleeping on the couch."

Maggie laughed, and then said, "Yes, well, Laura and I didn't want Sandy to feel bad if we had dates and she didn't, what with Jake being in Afghanistan still, so we're all going stag together."

Ginger patted her hand. "That's nice. So, show me your dress."

"It's nothing," Maggie said. "Very plain."

"Show me," Ginger insisted.

"Fine," Maggie said. She led Ginger to the storeroom where she'd put aside dresses for herself, Sandy and Laura. She opened the door and pulled out the one she'd chosen.

It was exactly as she had described. Very plain. It was olive in color with long sleeves and came up to her collarbone in front.

"Um." Ginger frowned while she considered the dress. "You're going for a puritan look?"

Then Maggie turned it around and showed off the completely cutaway back, and Ginger's eyes went wide.

"Too daring?" Maggie asked.

"Sam is going to keel over dead—dead, I tell you."

"You probably shouldn't look so delighted when you say that," Maggie said.

"I can't help it," Ginger said. "After the night we saw him carrying those flowers and I was so sure they were for you, well, like I told Roger, I think he chickened out. And this dress . . . oh, honey, this dress is going to bring him to his knees."

"I really don't care what Sam Collins thinks of my dress," Maggie said.

"Oh, girlfriend, you are the worst liar ever," Ginger said.

"Only when it comes to Sam," Maggie admitted. "I'm really working on it."

"Work harder," Ginger said.

The night of the Madison ball was a flurry of activity at the Gerber house. The small house had only two bathrooms and three women all trying to get ready at the same time caused a traffic jam in front of the only full-length mirror.

Maggie kept her look simple to match her gown. She blew out her shoulder-length auburn hair and wore simple black pumps with a matching black clutch purse. She had also grabbed a black cashmere wrap to cover up her back from the cold and to keep on if she chickened out on her big reveal.

Her dress had one button at the top of her back and then cut away all the way to the bottom of her spine, where it clung to the curve of her behind and then flared out in a floor length skirt. She had never worn anything this daring in her entire life, and she didn't know if she could carry it off.

She cuddled with Josh in his adorable charcoal gray suit with a white dress shirt and navy blue bow tie. He looked as handsome as his father, Jake, and Maggie wished for the millionth time that Jake could be here to see his boy.

She ruffled his hair and read *Choo Choo* by Virginia Lee Burton. She had read it to him so many times that she didn't even have to look at the pages to read the story, and her mind drifted. She wondered who Sam would be taking to the ball tonight and then tried to convince herself that she didn't care.

"We're ready," Laura and Sandy said as they stepped into the living room together.

Sandy twirled around in her deep purple sheath gown, and said, "What do you think, Josh-by-gosh?"

"Mommy beautiful," Josh said as his eyes went big.

"And me?" Laura asked as she twirled. She was wearing a poppy red gown that was bright enough to complement her light auburn hair, which she wore in an updo that made her look even more mature than her nineteen years, and Maggie felt her chest clutch tight. It seemed like just yesterday that Laura had been in pigtails and flouncy skirts.

"You both look stunning," Maggie said. She rose from the couch and turned to grab her wrap, and Laura let out a low whistle.

"Mom!" Laura gaped. "That's like Lauren Bacall sexy."

"You think?" she asked. "Am I too old? Can I carry it off? Should I change?"

"Don't you dare!" Sandy said. "You look breathtaking."

"Thank you," she said. She trusted the girls to tell her if she was inappropriate; still, she was grateful for her wrap.

Maggie blew out a breath as she draped the soft cashmere around her shoulders. She didn't have to take it off, she reminded herself. Leading the way out, she waited for the others and then locked the door behind them as they headed to the ball.

Bianca had arranged for valet parking, so Maggie handed over the keys to her Volvo station wagon to a young man in a crisp black jacket and tie.

Topiary bushes decorated in white lights lined the steps to the large front doors. The doors were open, and Bianca Madison stood there in a strapless pewter gown with her dark hair swept up to the crown of her head and styled with a cascade of curls trailing down her back. She looked radiant, and Maggie wondered if it was because Max Button stood at her side in a black tuxedo with a matching pewter pocket square.

Bianca turned to Max and whispered something in his ear, and he gave her a smile of such brilliance that Maggie caught her breath. Had it really been just six months ago that he'd been serving ice cream at the Frosty Freeze while wearing a faded Yoo-hoo T-shirt and khaki shorts?

"Max!" Laura cried as she spied her former math tutor. She tripped up the stairs and hugged him and then Bianca, and gushed, "You two look amazing."

They both blushed and returned the compliment. Sandy ushered Josh, who was enthralled with the white lights on the bushes, up the steps, and more hugs were exchanged.

Finally, it was Maggie's turn. She kissed Bianca's cheek and then hugged Max.

"I'm so proud of you," she whispered to Max. He grinned, and she asked, "You're happy?"

He nodded, looking choked up. "I didn't think I could ever be this happy."

"I'm so glad," Maggie said.

"Me, too," he said. He reached out a hand and took Bianca's in his, giving it a squeeze. She glanced back from where she was greeting the next guests, and the smile she gave him was dazzling.

Maggie beamed at him and followed her family into the main room. There was a coat-check station, but Maggie opted to keep her wrap on. They followed the sound of music and laughter down the short hallway to the enormous ballroom.

The doors were open, and the room was already filling up. Tables were set around the room for older guests to sit, and the dance floor was crowded with younger guests dancing to the music from the band at the end of the room.

Garlands of pine had been strung across the massive ceiling, and paper lanterns in shades of red, green, gold and silver in all different sizes were strung all along the garlands, giving the room a soft and festive glow.

"Oh, wow," Laura said, taking it all in.

"Wow, indeed," Maggie agreed. "I can't believe Bianca managed all of this in just one week."

"Laura, come dance with me." Aaron Lancaster, looking very dashing in a dark suit and tie, appeared and held out a hand to her. Laura grabbed his hand and the two of them strode out to the floor.

Maggie felt someone approach her side and turned to see Ginger there.

"He looks just like his daddy did at our prom twenty-something years ago," Ginger said. "And Laura looks like you."

"Except," Maggie began and Ginger said with her, "she has Charlie's eyes."

Josie Belle

They smiled at each another.

"Oh, Ginger, where did the time go?" Maggie asked.

"I don't know," Ginger said with a shake of her head. Then she straightened up, and said, "Uh-oh, don't look now."

"Don't look at what?" Maggie asked. She turned to see what Ginger was looking at.

"What do you not understand about *don't look*?" Ginger asked, turning to face her. "Sam Collins is here."

"Oh." Maggie turned her head away. She focused on the dancers even though it about killed her not to check out Sam. She tried to make her voice sound casual when she asked, "So, who did he bring with him?"

Chapter 7

Ginger was quiet for so long that Maggie feared the worst.

"Do not tell me that he brought Summer Phillips," she said.

"No," Ginger's voice was pensive. "He seems to be alone."

"Alone? Really?"

Ginger grinned at her. "When are you going to admit that you like him?"

Maggie turned away. "I—"

"Oh, please," Ginger waved a hand at her. "I'm your best friend. I know you."

"Ugh, can we not talk about it now?"

"Okay, but just for tonight," Ginger said. "Tomorrow I thumb-wrestle you into admitting it."

Maggie laughed. "Deal."

"Something is going on with Sam, though," Ginger said. "He's just hanging around the front door like he's waiting for something."

"Or someone." Maggie sighed.

Mercifully, her phone rang, and she fished it out of her clutch. She checked the caller ID and was surprised to see Sandy's husband Jake's number pop up.

"Hello?" she answered. The band and crowd noise made it impossible to hear. "Hello, Jake?"

"Aunt Maggie," his low voice was just a rumble.

She stuck her finger in her ear and signaled to Ginger that she was going to duck out to take the call.

She stepped through one set of French doors that opened out onto a large veranda. A fire pit was at one end and heaters warmed spots along the balcony, which was decorated with more twinkling white lights and pine boughs.

"Jake, can you hear me?"

"I can hear you," he laughed. "Can you hear me?"

"Loud and clear," she said. "Oh, Jake, I wish you were here. Sandy looks amazing, and Josh is so handsome in his little suit."

"Oh, do me a favor and take a picture of them and send it to me, would you?" he asked.

"Definitely," Maggie agreed. "Did you want me to go get Sandy? I know she'd love to talk to you."

"I'd like to," he said. "But first, could you do me a big favor?"

"Anything," Maggie said. Jake's voice was gruffer than usual, and she suspected he was feeling low to be missing the holiday festivities with his family. "You're all right, aren't you? You weren't wounded were you?"

"No!" he said right away. "Nothing like that. I just miss my family."

"Oh, Jake," Maggie sighed. "What can I do to help?"

"Is there a band there?" he asked.

"Yes."

"Do you suppose you could ask them to play 'Unforgettable' by Irving Gordon?"

Maggie felt her throat constrict. "Your wedding song. Oh, Jake, that's so romantic."

"Yeah, I want Sandy to know I'm thinking of her."

"Will do," Maggie said. "Should I have her call you after?"

"Yeah," he said. "That'd be good."

"Okay, Jake, I'm on it. Take care of you," she said.

"I will," he agreed. "And Maggie, thanks."

Maggie put her phone back in her purse and blew out a breath. She really liked that boy. She hurried into the ballroom and signaled to the bandleader that she had a request.

He was a good-looking, older gentleman with thick white hair. Maggie whispered her request in his ear, and he gave her a warm smile.

Maggie made her way around the dance floor back to Ginger's side.

"Who was that?" Ginger asked.

"Jake."

"Sandy's Jake? Is he all right?"

"He's fine," Maggie assured her.

The band was winding down its song, and Sandy and Josh joined them. Maggie dipped her head at Sandy and put a finger to her lips. Ginger nodded in understanding.

"Ladies and gentleman, we have a special request," the

bandleader announced. He looked at Maggie, and she smiled her encouragement. "This next song goes out to Sandy from her loving husband, Jake."

The band kicked in and the bandleader, in a voice reminiscent of Nat King Cole, crooned "Unforgettable" into the microphone. Sandy's eyes went wide, and she blushed as the entire room turned to look at her.

"But how?" Sandy asked.

"He just phoned it in," Maggie said.

Sandy's eyes were watery, and she nodded as if this was something she would expect Jake to do. She held her hand out to Josh.

"Will you come and dance to Mommy and Daddy's song with me?"

Josh gave her a shy smile and put his hand in hers. Together they strode out to the empty dance floor and everyone watched as the mother and son held hands and moved in a slow circle. Josh grinned up at his mom as she twirled him, and then he giggled.

"Adorable," Ginger whispered.

Maggie turned to agree and caught sight of Sam, looking knee-wiltingly handsome in a black tuxedo and bow tie. His gaze met hers, and then he turned and hustled out the door into the hallway.

She wondered what that meant. Maybe his date had arrived. Curious to see who she might be, Maggie stood up on her tiptoes. In moments, Sam returned, and when Maggie saw who entered the ballroom behind him, she gasped and clutched Ginger's arm.

Ginger took one look at Maggie's face, and then she spun to see what Maggie was looking at. She let out a muffled shriek, which caused everyone around them to slowly turn to the door.

Still in his fatigues, Jake strode into the ballroom. Other than the sound of the band playing, the entire room went silent. As if sensing something was happening, Sandy looked up from Josh. She stumbled to a halt and pressed her right hand over her mouth.

Josh looked up at his mother and then spun around. His blue eyes went wide, and he yelled, "Daddy!"

Then he started to run as fast as his chubby little legs could carry him. Jake knelt down and scooped up his son, clutching him close.

"Daddy! You're here!" Josh cried as he patted his father's cheeks as if to make sure he was real, while Jake planted kisses all over his son's face.

Jake shifted him onto his hip and strode out onto the dance floor. Sandy stood transfixed, staring at her two men. The tears were coursing down her cheeks and sobs rocked her shoulders.

Jake opened up his other arm and swept her into a family hug. The bandleader's voice faded out, and the band played a hushed version of the song while Jake hugged Sandy close and kissed her lips and hair. When she pulled back she was still crying, and Josh reached forward and cupped her face, and said, "It's okay, Mommy. Daddy's home."

Sandy kissed her son and her husband, and the three of them continued their dance. Maggie wasn't sure who started it, but someone began to applaud and soon the whole room was clapping and cheering and there wasn't a dry eye in the house.

"Oh my god, look at me," Ginger said. "I'm a mess."

Maggie sniffed and nodded. "I'll go fetch us some tissue."

She turned to leave and found Sam and Roger standing behind them. Sam handed her a handkerchief, and Roger did the same for Ginger.

"Thank you," Maggie said as she blotted the skin beneath her eyes and the tip of her nose.

Maggie had never been a pretty crier. Her nose and eyes turned bright red and her skin got all blotchy. She lowered her face and let her hair hang in front of her in an attempt to cover the damage.

Sam leaned close, and asked, "Are you all right?"

"Just emotional," she said. The knot in her throat was still tight and her voice came out gruff.

Sam smiled at her, and Maggie suddenly remembered that he had been loitering by the door and in the hall.

"Did you know Jake was coming back tonight?" she asked.

Sam pursed his lips and whistled while studying the garland above their heads.

"You did, didn't you?" she asked.

"His dad might have called the station to see if I could pick him up at the airport with a squad car to get him here in time," Sam said.

"Aw." Maggie felt her eyes well up again. "That was so nice of you."

"Jake's dad was the QB of our high school team when I was a freshman," he said. "He's a good man."

"Is he here?" she asked, scanning the crowd.

"He and his wife are driving up from Florida as we speak," he said. "They're excited to see their boy, but they knew Jake wanted to surprise Laura and Josh."

"Well, it was an amazing surprise," Maggie said. She put her hand on his arm, and said, "Thank you."

Sam looked like he was about to say something, but just then the song ended and Laura popped out of the crowd. She grabbed Maggie's hand and dragged her out onto the dance floor to go give Jake a welcome-home hug.

Maggie cupped Jake's face and kissed both of his cheeks. He grinned at her in just the same way Josh did when he was really happy, and Maggie felt her heart lift.

"Welcome home, Jake," she said.

"Thanks, Aunt Maggie." He grinned, and Maggie let Laura have her turn.

Turning away from the group, Maggie dreaded to think of what she must look like. She decided to scoot to the bathroom and attempt some damage control. Plus, that would give her a few minutes to get it together. She was still feeling watery and was afraid she'd start bawling again at the sight of the reunited family.

Maggie slipped out of the ballroom and into the hallway. The bathroom that she was familiar with was locked. She decided to try farther down the hall. In a house this size there had to be another bathroom. She looked in on a small study and a coat closet. She heard voices coming from behind the next door, and she thought maybe she could ask there for directions to the bathroom.

The door was ajar, so she glanced around it before pushing it open, not wanting to interrupt if the catering staff were having a meeting.

The voices kept on in a rush, however, as they obviously didn't notice her at the door.

"This can't go on, Diane," Michael Claramotta said.

Maggie felt her heart thump hard in her chest. Joanne's husband Michael and Diane Jenkins, his new hire, were standing at the back of the room. Diane had her arms crossed over her middle as if she were upset and trying to hold it in. Michael looked distressed—not angry, but very agitated.

"Don't you see?" he asked. "I have to think about Joanne and the baby. I can't let this hurt them."

Diane gave a small nod, and her voice was wooden when she said, "I understand."

"It just can't go on," he said. "It's not right. Not for you. Not for anyone."

Diane sobbed and nodded, and Michael reached out and pulled her close in a reassuring hug.

"You're going to be okay," he whispered against her hair. "I promise."

Maggie slowly backed away from the door. Her throat was dry, and she felt as if someone had reached into her chest and tied her insides into a fancy sailor's knot.

"Maggie," a voice called her name.

Maggie spun away from the door and turned to see Joanne, barreling down on her and just seconds from walking in on her husband with his arms around another woman.

Chapter 8

"Joanne!" she cried. "Just the person I need. Tell me, is my makeup a wreck? I was looking for a bathroom because the other one was occupied."

Joanne gave her a weak smile. "Oh, that was me. The baby queasies hit hard, but at least I didn't get sick."

"Oh, you poor thing," Maggie commiserated, looping her arm through her friend's and leading her back toward the ballroom.

"Your makeup looks fine," Joanne said. She studied Maggie's face. "No runs. No drips."

"How about blotches?" Maggie asked, casting a quick glance over her shoulder to see that neither Michael nor Diane had appeared.

"They're fading," Joanne assured her. And the lighting is so dim, I'm sure no one will notice."

"Thanks."

"Hey, have you seen Michael?" Joanne asked. "He was waiting for me in the hallway, but I lost him."

"Oh, hey, look!" Maggie replied, pretending she hadn't heard Joanne's question. "There's Claire and Pete."

Claire looked stunning in her bright blue gown, and Pete Daniels stood beside her, looking quite dashing in his tuxedo. He also looked completely besotted with Claire. Maggie smiled. That was exactly how it should be.

They were standing with Ginger and Roger, and Maggie steered Joanne in their direction, hoping to keep her from thinking about where Michael had wandered off to.

Maggie supposed a tough-love sort of friend would have let Joanne walk in on Michael and Diane, but given how hard it had been for Joanne to get pregnant, Maggie didn't want her to get upset. And Maggie knew that if Joanne saw her husband, the love of her life since she was a kid, having a whispered conversation while embracing a cute young thing, she was going to be upset.

She supposed their conversation could have been about a variety of things, even though it had sounded really incriminating. Maybe there was a logical reason behind the words they had exchanged. She sifted through what she remembered.

"It just can't go on," Michael had said. *"It's not right. Not for you. Not for anyone."*

What couldn't go on? That's what Maggie wanted to know. Was it something happening between Michael and Diane? Was it something Diane was doing at the deli? Maggie knew it was none of her business, and yet, Joanne was her friend. How could she not speculate and wonder?

"Mean-girl alert," Laura said as she and Aaron rejoined the group.

"What?" Maggie asked. "Where?"

"Britney and company have Diane surrounded," Laura said.

"Not for long," Aaron said. He emitted a sharp whistle and in moments his brothers, Byron, Caleb and Dante, made their way through the crowd toward him.

Maggie glanced back at Diane, who was no longer with Michael, and sure enough, Britney Bergstrom, who had wanted the gown that Maggie rented to Diane, had a posse of friends circling Diane. One of them was pointing at Diane and laughing. From the malicious look on her face, it was obvious that she was being nasty.

Despite what Maggie had overheard between Michael and Diane, she felt her blood boil. She loathed bullies.

Maggie went to step forward, but Ginger stayed her with a hand on her arm. She pointed, and Maggie saw Ginger's four boys and Laura moving toward Diane, effectively surrounding her.

Caleb, Ginger's third-born son, held out his arm to Diane, and she clutched it with obvious relief as he led her out onto the dance floor. Meanwhile, Laura and Aaron stood like sentries with their arms crossed over their chests, glaring at Britney until she and her friends scurried away.

"It's moments like this that I am most proud of our children," Maggie said.

"Agreed," Ginger said with a smile. "They are good people."

When Britney and her crowd left, Aaron and Laura

joined Diane and Caleb on the dance floor while Byron went in search of his girlfriend and Dante, the youngest of the Lancaster boys, looked to be heading back to a cluster of his friends by the buffet table.

"Oh, would you look at that?" Ginger said.

Maggie whipped her head around to follow Ginger's stunned gaze to the door. She felt her own jaw drop.

Summer Phillips was standing in the doorway with her hand on the arm of Tyler Fawkes. To say that they were a striking couple was an understatement. Tyler had squeezed his considerable girth into a white tuxedo with a black shirt, open at the throat, very John Travolta in *Saturday Night Fever*.

But Summer. Summer was the topper. Pink sparkles caught the eye, but then it was hard to decide where to look. In what appeared to be formal wear à la Frederick's of Hollywood, Summer wore a dress, if it could be called such, that consisted of two strips of narrow sparkly fabric that crisscrossed over her bosom, leaving her entire upper torso bare. Her skirt was more of the same glittery pink fabric but sported a thigh-high slit in the front. She towered over Tyler in silver platform sandals, and her faux blonde hair was teased up to add another few inches as it had been styled into huge roll on top of her head and was held in place by a sparkling tiara.

Everyone in the room turned to take in the couple, and even the band stumbled for a note or two. To put it mildly, Summer was a showstopper. She preened under the attention and scanned the room. When her eyes lit upon Maggie, she gave her a cat-that-ate-the-canary smile and made her way over to their group.

"Summer." Ginger greeted her as she approached. "Funny. I didn't think you were on the guest list."

"Don't need to be," she said. "I'm Tyler's date."

Tyler hadn't taken his eyes off of Summer's chest, and Maggie was pretty sure he hadn't heard a word she'd said.

"Isn't that right, Tyler?" Summer asked. "Tyler, eyes up here!"

Summer pinched his arm, and Tyler said, "Ouch!" and snapped his eyes up to hers.

"Yes, dearest," he said.

Summer cast them a self-satisfied smirk. Then she turned her gaze on Maggie, and it glowed with triumph.

"What, did the Amish have a fire sale?" she asked as she took in Maggie's gown with obvious distaste.

Maggie glanced down at her gown. She was covered from neck to ankle, and she hadn't taken off her wrap yet, which made her look as bundled up as a demure grandmother.

"Why you—" Ginger sputtered in Maggie's defense, but a deep voice cut her off.

"Maggie, there you are," the voice said from behind her. "I believe this dance is mine."

Maggie turned her head to see Sam standing behind her. She had no doubt that he had stepped in to keep the peace. She would have protested that she had no intention of scuffling with Summer at the ball, but she figured she'd just take the out Sam was offering and for once keep her mouth shut.

"Go on," Joanne said. "I'll hold your wrap."

Before Maggie could protest, Joanne snapped it off her, and Maggie felt the cool evening air hit her back with a slap.

A breath hissed from behind her, and Maggie looked over her shoulder to see Sam taking in her bare back. She felt an embarrassed heat rise to her cheeks, but then his gaze met hers and it smoldered.

Without saying a word, he held out his hand to her. Maggie took it and Sam twirled her onto the dance floor as if they had been dancing together forever. It occurred to Maggie that in some ways they had been dancing close and then darting away from each other all their lives.

The band was playing "It Had to Be You" by Isham Jones and Gus Kahn. They were playing it slow, and as Sam waltzed her around the floor it was hard to catch her breath with his body so close to hers and her insides fluttering as if a thousand feathers were tickling her.

"Nice dress," Sam said. His hand slid down her back from her shoulder blades to the base of her spine.

"Thank you," Maggie said. She felt unaccountably shy and hyperaware of his callused hand on her exposed skin.

Sam surprised her by twirling her, and Maggie laughed as he reeled her back in again. He grinned at her, pulling her close.

"I didn't know you were such a good dancer," she said, trying to keep the conversation light and normal.

"I'm feeling inspired," he said.

Maggie tilted her head, not understanding.

"I want to show off my incredibly sexy partner," he said.

Maggie felt her face get hot. "Won't your date be annoyed?"

"No," he said. "The lovely lady I wanted to take already had plans, so I came alone."

"Summer dumped you for Tyler, huh?" Maggie said. "Bummer."

Sam tipped back his head and laughed. He was stunningly handsome when he laughed, and Maggie felt her breath catch as her heart hiccupped in her chest.

Sam slowed them down and pulled her even closer and, as the bandleader crooned the last line of the song, Sam whispered the line in her ear, "It had to be you."

He pulled back to gaze at her and, for once in her life, Maggie found she was speechless. As the band ended the song, Sam led her to one side of the room and right out the French doors onto the patio.

The cold air felt good against her heated skin. She stepped out of Sam's arms, but he held on to her hand and led her to a dark and unpopulated corner of the balcony.

Maggie shivered, but it wasn't from the cold. She felt as if this moment between her and Sam had been coming forever.

"Here," he said as he shrugged out of his jacket and wrapped it around her shoulders.

"Thanks, but I'm not cold," she said.

"You're shivering." He shook his head, obviously not getting it.

Maggie blew out a breath. How thick could the man be?

"Sam, I—" she began, while he said, "Maggie, I—"

"Oh, sorry, you go ahead," she said.

"No, ladies first," he said.

"All right," she said.

Maggie stared at the man in front of her. At various times in her life she'd wanted to back over him with her car, split a pizza together and go skinny-dipping with him. It was not hard to discern which of those three she felt like doing now, since his blue eyes gleamed at her and his very trim and muscular body was defined by the moonlight in high-def under his white dress shirt.

"Sam, I—" she began again.

"Oh, hell," he said. "I can't take this."

Maggie didn't have a chance to catch her breath as Sam's hands framed her face, holding her still while his mouth descended on hers in a kiss that was so hot it left scorch marks on everything around them.

It took Maggie only a moment to realize that this was Sam's way of telling her how he felt. Before he could pull away, she knew it was her turn to be clear, and she fisted his shirt in her hands and refused to let him go. She felt him go still for just a second while he processed the fact that she was kissing him back, and then his arms dropped to her hips and slid up her back to pull her closer.

When they finally pulled apart, they were both breathing heavy and Sam's jacket had dropped to the ground. Maggie rested her head on his shoulder, listening to his heart pound in time with her own.

Sam's hand slid up her back to play with the ends of her hair. "So . . ."

Maggie leaned back and looked at his face. Had he always been this impossibly handsome?

"So, I know we are trying to be friends, but I don't want to be friends anymore," she said.

The look he gave her was intense, as if he was afraid there was an option that he hadn't thought of and he didn't want to get blasted.

"Well, I don't kiss my enemies like that," he said.

"Me neither," Maggie said.

"So that leaves . . ."

"Dating," she said. "I'm afraid if you're going to kiss me like that, we're just going to have to start dating."

Sam let out a whoop and spun her around, making Maggie laugh. Then he stopped and studied her with a look that made her insides knot up.

"Really?" he asked.

Maggie met his gaze and grinned. "Yes."

Sam pulled her close and planted another bone-melting kiss on her.

"Good," he said. "But Maggie, you have to be sure."

"I am," she said. She did a quick check, and everything inside of her screamed that this was right. "I promise I am absolutely sure."

"Good," he said. He kissed her quickly. "Because I'm older and wiser now, and I'm going to be a lot harder to scrape off this time."

"No scraping, I promise," she said. "Can I ask you one thing?"

He nodded.

"A few weeks ago," she began and then paused. She felt like an idiot, but she had to know. If there was someone else he was interested in, she needed to know now before she got in too deep. "Right after I got out of the hospital, Ginger saw you coming down the street with flowers. Who were they for?"

"Ginger saw me, huh?" he asked.

"Yep," Maggie said. "In fact, we all did."

"They were for you," he said. He looked embarrassed, and Maggie frowned.

"Me?"

"Yeah, but on my way I ran into Pete Daniels, also with flowers for you," he said, looking annoyed. "You and I had agreed to be friends, so I thought you had moved on with Pete, and I didn't want to mess it up for you."

"Oh," she said. She put a hand on the side of his face. "I think that's the nicest thing anyone's ever done for me. Totally stupid, but really nice."

"Stupid?" he asked. Then his hand quickly found the tickle spot on her side, and he was merciless.

Maggie yelped and giggled as his fingers teased her the same way he had he had over twenty years before.

"Uncle!" Maggie cried. "Not stupid. More like wonderful, charming and gallant."

Sam immediately stopped tickling her and pulled her close. "Come dance with me."

Maggie glanced up at him and grinned. "We could do that, or we could stay out here by ourselves."

Sam placed a quick kiss on her mouth and stooped to retrieve his coat. "No, I can't trust myself alone with you for much longer. Besides, I have been waiting for over twenty years to show you off as my girlfriend, and I will not be denied."

Maggie hadn't thought it was possible to love Sam Collins more than she had when she was a teenager. She realized as he led her back into the ballroom and looked at her as if she was the only person who mattered that she had been wrong—so wrong.

Chapter 9

The night passed in a blur. Maggie gave Jake the keys to her car so he could take Sandy and Josh home early, as the family wanted to spend some time alone. Sam said he would take Maggie and Laura home when they were ready, but Laura was dancing with all of her old high school friends and Maggie, well, she was just happy to be with Sam.

They seldom left the dance floor, and Maggie could hear people whispering as they danced on by. Sam didn't care, and he seemed determined not to let her out of his sight. In fact, the only person he let cut in was Max Button.

"So, you and Sam, huh?" Max asked as he spun Maggie around the floor.

What Max lacked in coordination, he made up for in enthusiasm, and so long as Maggie kept her toes out of stomping range, they moved pretty smoothly.

"Is it shocking?" she asked.

"No," he said. "I think everyone in town figured it was just a matter of time. Well, everyone except Pete, but he seems to have moved on."

Maggie followed Max's gaze to where Pete and Claire were dancing. Pete was telling jokes and Claire was laughing. They looked delighted with each other, and Maggie was relieved. She noticed Max's frown, however, and remembered that he had carried a torch for the librarian since she'd found him trying to live in the library when he was a young teen.

"Max, you can't deny Claire the same happiness you've found with Bianca," she said.

"I don't," he said with a sigh. "It's just that I'll always feel protective of her. She saved my life when she found me in the library."

"Claire is an extraordinary woman," Maggie agreed. "But I think Pete knows that, too."

Max glanced at the happy couple and back at Maggie. He gave her a small smile.

"Yeah, Pete seems like a good guy, and I do want Claire to be happy, but you never get over your first crush."

Maggie scanned the ballroom until she found Sam leaning against the wall with Ginger's husband Roger at his side. Roger was talking and Sam was nodding, but he had his attention trained on Maggie. When their gazes met, he gave her a wicked wink. Maggie felt her face grow hot, and she turned her attention back to Max before she tripped.

"No, I don't suppose you ever do," she said.

When the dance ended, Max stopped right in front of Sam and handed her over. Maggie glanced between the two of them and got the feeling that this had been arranged.

Before she could question it, Sam spun her back out onto the floor.

Being in Sam's arms made Maggie forget everything; her anxiety about her shop, hosting Christmas dinner, even the scene she'd witnessed between Michael Claramotta and Diane Jenkins. She did note that Michael spent the rest of the evening with Joanne. But even that barely registered, as she was completely engaged in being with Sam.

After the band played its final song for the night, Sam took Maggie and Laura home. His personal vehicle was a roomy SUV, and he opened the passenger doors for Laura and Maggie before circling the car and getting into the driver's seat.

They left the mansion behind, waving to Bianca and Max as they went. When they reached the end of the driveway, Laura's head popped up between Sam and Maggie.

"So, Sam," she said. "What are you plans for Christmas Eve?"

"I'm on duty," he said. "I figured my deputies could use the holiday off, so I took patrol duty, and Deputy Wilson is manning the station."

"But you'll take a break for dinner, right?" she asked.

Maggie turned her head to stare at her daughter. What was she up to?

"Yes, we're allowed to eat," Sam said.

"Great, then you have to stop by our house for dinner," she said. "Five o'clock, okay?"

Sam gave Maggie a sideways glance and she shrugged, and said, "We'll have plenty of food."

He studied her for a second and then he smiled. "That'd be nice. Thank you."

Maggie felt her face grow warm at the thought of having Sam over for Christmas Eve dinner with her mother and sister in town. Her mother was one of the few people who knew that Sam had broken her heart. Was twenty years enough time for her mother to let it go? The thought was alarming.

Laura sat back with a self-satisfied smile, and Maggie shook her head. At least she knew how Laura felt about Sam.

As Sam pulled into the driveway, Laura sprang out of the car, calling, "Thanks, Sam!" over her shoulder. She keyed into the house before Sam even had Maggie's door open.

"Subtle, isn't she?" Maggie asked.

Sam took her hand and helped her down. As they walked up to her front door, he kept his hand on her lower back, just under her wrap. For a second, Maggie wished her house wasn't quite so full. She would have liked to invite Sam in.

At the door, she turned to face him. "Thanks for the ride."

"Maggie," he said. He sounded reluctant, and Maggie wondered if he was about to duck out of Christmas Eve dinner, and she couldn't blame him, although she would be disappointed.

"Yes," she said.

"About Laura's invitation," he said.

"You don't have to come," she said. "I know that the holidays are a time for family, and—"

"Oh, I want to come," he interrupted. "But I can see where Laura, who I really like by the way, maneuvered you into inviting me."

"And I am really glad she did," Maggie said.

"Are you sure?" he asked.

"Yes," she said. She wrapped her arms around Sam's

neck. "Since you have to work, please come have dinner with my crazy family. I promise I'll make it worth your while."

At that, Sam's eyebrows lifted, and he asked, "Oh, really?"

Maggie laughed. "I meant with ham, but there's room for negotiation."

"And I do love negotiating with you," Sam said. And then he kissed her.

Maggie's last thought as she waved good-bye to him through the front window and toddled off to bed was that she had to get to More than Meats first thing in the morning and order a bigger ham.

Dancing the night away had left Maggie bone-weary but heart-light. She and Laura cranked the holiday tunes as they reworked their displays for the crush of last-minute holiday shoppers that they were hoping for. Of course, with the majority of Bianca's gowns having been sold for the ball, Maggie knew she could get through the holiday without selling another thing and she'd be fine. It was a good feeling.

Maggie left Laura to tend the shop while she hurried over to More than Meats to revise her ham order. She tried to imagine what her mother and sister would say when they arrived to find not just Jake but Sam, too, at the dinner table. They had been male-light for several years, so this was going to be an adjustment.

When Maggie arrived at the deli, she was surprised to find that it was still dark and locked. The closed sign hung in the window, and she got a sick feeling in her stomach.

Michael never missed a day at work, ever. What if something was wrong with Joanne and the baby?

She hurriedly fished her phone out of her purse and called Joanne. It rang three times before Joanne's chipper voice answered.

"Maggie, I've been dying to call you and ask about Sam." Joanne started right in. "So, what happened?"

"Um." Maggie was so surprised that Joanne had answered that she couldn't get her thoughts to process the question. "Joanne, is Michael with you?"

"No, I'm just leaving the hardware store," she said. "They are having a paint sale, so I picked a nice gender-neutral green to paint the nursery. Green stimulates brain activity, you know."

"No, I didn't," Maggie said.

She hesitated. Should she say anything about the shop being closed? She glanced back at the dark windows and the locked door. This felt wrong. She had to tell Joanne.

"Maggie, are you there?" Joanne asked. "Hello? Can you hear me?"

"Joanne, I'm standing in front of the deli, and it's closed and locked. Is Michael away today?"

"What? No, he went into work early as usual," Joanne said. "Are the lights on? Maybe he just forgot to unlock the front door."

"No, no lights are on," Maggie said.

"Well, that's weird. Wait for me," Joanne said. "I'll be there in five."

She was there in three. Her SUV stopped at the curb with a lurch, and she bolted out of the driver's side door. Her eyes were wide with worry as she strode toward Maggie.

"No sign of him?"

"None." Maggie shook her head.

Joanne tried the front door as if she just had to check. Maggie understood. She would have done the same.

"Maybe he's in the office in back," Joanne said. "Maybe he just forgot to open."

The two women hurried around the building. Maggie couldn't shake the bad feeling she had about this. What if they walked in on Michael and Diane? No, she pushed the thought aside. Despite what she had seen at the ball, she didn't believe that Michael would cheat on Joanne—not now, not ever.

The alley was made up of tall red-brick buildings. Dumpsters were scattered behind the backs of the buildings, and even in the chilly weather the cement gave off a whiff of decaying garbage.

Joanne tried the back door. It was unlocked. She gave Maggie a worried look.

"Michael always keeps the back door locked," she said.

Joanne turned the knob and pulled the door open. She stepped into the large storeroom at the back of the shop. This was where deliveries were dropped off. Several walk-in freezers and refrigerators filled this space, which led to the kitchen where the specialty items for the deli were made.

"Michael?" Joanne called. "Are you here?"

There was no answer. As they walked into the kitchen, Joanne went rigid and shrieked, causing Maggie to jump.

"Michael!" Joanne cried, and she dropped to her knees on the floor where her husband lay, his head in a pool of blood.

"Don't move him," Maggie ordered as she dropped down

beside her friend. She reached for his wrist and checked his pulse. It was faint but still there. She fumbled with her phone. She called the first person who came to mind.

"Hello," Dr. Franklin answered on the first ring.

"Doc, I'm at More than Meats," Maggie said. "Joanne and I just got here and we found Michael on the kitchen floor. He's unconscious and his head is resting in a pool of blood. Can you come?"

"Don't move him," Doc ordered. "I'm at the office and can be there in a few minutes. I'll have Cheryl call for an ambulance."

Maggie ended the call. Joanne was sobbing softly beside her. She was holding her husband's hand and talking to him.

"I'm here, Michael," she said. "Don't you worry. I'll take care of you."

Maggie felt her throat get tight. She put her arm around her friend and said, "Don't worry. Head gashes cause a lot of blood loss but usually they're more messy than dangerous." Maggie didn't mention that head injuries could be very serious. She wanted to buoy her friend not sink her.

Joanne glanced around the room. "What could have . . . I mean . . . do you think he tripped and cracked his head?"

"I don't know," Maggie said. She glanced at the floor to see if there was a puddle of water, a grease stain, a stray ice cube or anything else that would have caused him to slip. There was nothing. The linoleum looked perfectly clean, which was not surprising, as Michael kept a scrupulously tidy kitchen.

Maggie's eyes moved away from Michael's feet and across the floor. She saw the string of an apron on the ground, and she craned her neck to see if that was what he had tripped on. She couldn't quite see around the large work island, so she leaned forward. A mop of blonde hair was on the floor.

She jumped to her feet and hurried around the workstation. Every instinct inside of her told her that this was going to be bad, but she forced herself to continue forward.

"Maggie, what is it?" Joanne cried.

Maggie couldn't speak. A small whimper came out of her mouth as she knelt down and saw the ties of a white butcher's apron were tied tightly, way too tightly, around Diane Jenkins's throat.

She loosened the ties where they dug into the skin and pressed her fingers just under Diane's ear. Her skin was cold to the touch, her face was a mottled red color and her body was stiff and unresponsive.

Maggie placed her hand on the young woman's chest. It didn't rise and fall. She moved her hand in front of Diane's mouth, but no breath was emitted. She felt no heartbeat, and Diane's eyes were closed as if she'd just decided to take a nap on the kitchen floor, but she hadn't.

Maggie glanced around the workstation and met Joanne's horrified gaze.

"It's Diane. She's dead."

Chapter 10

Maggie fumbled for her phone. Her fingers were shaking so hard that she could barely press the numbers for the police.

"St. Stanley Sheriff's Department, Deputy Wilson speaking," a woman's voice answered.

"Dot, it's Maggie," she said. Her voice was faint, so she cleared her throat before she continued. "Is Sam there?"

"Maggie, are you all right?" Dot asked. "You sound awful."

"No, not all right," she said. "Need Sam."

"Hang on," Dot said.

Moments later Sam's voice was on the line.

"Maggie, what is it?"

"I'm at More than Meats," Maggie said. "Michael Claramotta is unconscious and his assistant Diane Jenkins is . . . oh, Sam . . . she's dead. I think she was strangled."

Maggie's voice broke, and she felt the dampness on her cheeks before she even realized she was crying.

"Are you all right?" Sam asked. "Is anyone else there?"

"Yes, I'm here with Joanne," she said. "I already called Doc about Michael. He's on his way and he sent an ambulance. I didn't see Diane until after."

"I'll be right there," Sam said. "I'm putting you back on with Dot. Don't hang up. Don't touch anything. Don't leave the kitchen."

"I won't," she promised.

Joanne was sobbing. She was still by Michael's side, holding his hand as if she were afraid he'd vanish on her if she let go.

"Maggie, it's Dot," Deputy Wilson said. "What's going on?"

Maggie told her just what she'd told Sam. Dot gave a low whistle.

"Sam just ran out of here. He should be there right away," Dot said. "Stay on the line with me."

"I will," Maggie said. She knew only minutes had passed since she'd called Doc, but it felt like an eternity.

The dining area out front seemed terribly quiet, and Maggie strained to hear if there was anyone out there moving among the tables.

"Do not even poke your head out that swinging door," Dot said. Her voice startled Maggie, and she sucked in a deep breath.

"I was not about to do that," she said.

"Uh-huh," Dot said. It didn't sound like she believed her.

A noise came from the storeroom, and Maggie glanced up to see Doc Franklin arrive with a pair of EMTs behind him.

"Doc Franklin is here with the paramedics," Maggie said.

"Okay, you can put the phone down if you have to," Dot said.

Doc bustled into the kitchen. The two EMTs knew him and deferred to him. He took the scene in at a glance, blanching at the sight of the woman beside Maggie.

"She's dead," Maggie said. "I found her after I called you."

"Start on him," Doc told the EMTs, and he came over and checked Diane's vitals, being careful to touch her as little as possible. In moments, he sat back on his heels, looking older than when he'd entered the room.

"You're right," he said. "There's nothing we can do for her."

He gave Maggie a sad nod and hurried back over to Michael. Maggie moved to stand beside Joanne, who had moved to give Doc and the EMTs room to work on her husband. Joanne was still crying, but it was silent now. The tears rolled down her face in an unending stream as she watched them work.

The back door was yanked open and Sam rushed in. He took one look at Maggie and snatched her into a hug, running his hands across her back and along her arms as if to reassure himself that she was okay.

"All right?" he asked.

She meant to say, "Fine," but the word stuck in her throat. It was a lie with barbs that hooked in and held on and she couldn't force it out. She was anything but all right.

Sam pulled back and looked at her. He studied her face, taking in the shock and horror. Then he kissed her forehead and squeezed her hands in his. The gesture comforted her.

"Dot, Sam's here," Maggie said into her phone.

"Good, you can end the call now," Dot said. Then her voice got soft, and she said, "Still, be careful, okay?"

"I will," Maggie said, and ended the call.

Sam stepped farther into the room. He saw Doc working on Michael and then moved around the workstation to Diane. Maggie saw him crouch down low. In moments he was back. His face was set in grim lines.

"We have to take Michael to the hospital," Doc said as he joined them.

"Any indication of what happened?" Sam asked.

"Severe head injury," Doc said. He looked worriedly at Joanne, and Maggie got the feeling he would have said more but he didn't want to distress her.

The EMTs brought in a backboard and strapped Michael in. Joanne, Maggie and Sam were all silent as they watched. Joanne pressed a hand over her mouth as if to keep her cries in, and Maggie put her arm around her friend's shoulders, trying to give her strength.

Doc looked at Maggie, and said, "I'll ride with him in the ambulance," he said. "You take Joanne in my car."

Maggie nodded and glanced at Sam.

"I'll secure the scene and get the county coroner out here. We'll talk later," he said. "Are you sure you can drive?"

"Yeah," Maggie said. She hoped he didn't see how badly her hands were shaking.

They stepped aside as the EMTs wheeled Michael out. Joanne hurried after them, and Doc took Maggie's place. He put his hand on Joanne's back and talked to her in that soothing way that only Doc had that made you feel like there was nothing in life that a bandage and a cherry lollipop couldn't fix.

Sam took Maggie's hand in his and they followed everyone out. Maggie was grateful for the support. The thought of what had happened here terrified her. A young woman dead and her friend's husband—scratch that; she considered Michael her friend as well—*her friend* unconscious.

"Call me from the hospital and let me know you're okay," Sam said.

"I will," Maggie said. "And, Sam, thanks."

He kissed her quickly on the mouth before helping her into the driver's seat of Doc's car while Doc helped Joanne into the passenger seat. Doc hurried into the ambulance, and they closed the door behind him. Giving Sam what she hoped was a brave smile, Maggie stomped on the gas and followed the ambulance at top speed to the nearby hospital.

As they zipped through town, Maggie patted Joanne's hand, noticing that she kept the other one firmly wrapped around her belly as if protecting her and Michael's baby from what was happening.

Maggie dropped Joanne off at the door right behind the ambulance and went to park the car. By the time she got into the emergency room, Michael had been wheeled into a room and Doc Franklin was in there conversing with several other people in white coats.

Joanne was standing outside the room. Her face was the picture of devastation as she stood almost pressed up to the glass, trying to be with her husband.

Maggie stood beside her. She couldn't think of any words of comfort that wouldn't sound hollow, so she said nothing. She remembered the night her husband, Charlie, had been killed. Laura had been a toddler, and Maggie had left her with her mother so that she could be at the hospital. It had been Ginger, pregnant with her second son, who stood beside her.

"I can't lose him, Maggie," Joanne's voice was just a whisper. "Do you know when I fell in love with him?"

"No," Maggie said, although she'd heard the story before.

"We were in second grade, and Michael gave me a silly paper valentine with a honeybee on it that asked, 'Will you bee mine?' and right then I knew I was going to marry him," she said. "He gave Violet Cosetti one that said, 'I choo-choo-choose you,' with a little train on it, but I took care of her with the threat of a knuckle sandwich for lunch if she didn't get away from my boyfriend."

Maggie felt a smile pull at her lips. She could just see New York City–bred Joanne staking her claim on her boy and not letting go.

"He hasn't been able to shake me loose since." Joanne sniffed.

Maggie immediately put her arm around her and pulled her close.

"Shh, it's going to be okay," she said. "Michael is young and strong and he'd never willingly leave you or the baby. You know that."

The door to their right opened and Doc Franklin came out. He was pale, and his white hair was standing in tufts like it always did at the end of the day or in times of extreme stress.

"Joanne," he said. "Michael is going to be taken for an MRI. It appears he's got some bleeding on the brain, and we're worried about the pressure. It looks like he's going to need some surgery, and the MRI will help us proceed with that."

"Oh no." Joanne pressed her fingers to her lips, which were quivering. "Can I see him before he goes?"

"Quickly," Doc said.

Maggie followed, standing just inside the open door while Joanne hurried to her husband's side.

"Now you listen to me, Michael Claramotta: The doctors are going to fix you up, and you're going to get well, because I—" Joanne's voice broke but she took a breath and forged on. "—because I love you, Michael. Since we were eight, there's never been anyone but you and—" Her voice broke again, and Maggie felt her own throat close up. She wanted to rush to her friend and hug her, but she waited. "—and I'll even let you name the baby, whatever you choose, even—oh, I can't believe I'm saying this—but even after your Uncle Sal, if that's what you want."

"We have to go now, Joanne," Doc Franklin said gently.

She nodded quickly and leaned over Michael, pressing her lips to his. "I love you."

They wheeled him out past Maggie, and she looked at Joanne, standing alone in the room, looking as lost and as scared as Maggie remembered being when she had lost her husband. She hoped, all the way down to her core, that Joanne and Michael's outcome was vastly different than her and Charlie's.

"Come on," she said. "Let's go find a place to wait."

Joanne nodded, tears streaming down her face, and they went in search of the waiting room.

Joanne sat with her hands clenched in her lap. Her eyes were closed, and Maggie knew that she was praying. Maggie didn't want to intrude, so she whispered that she was going to get them some coffee. Joanne nodded but kept her head bowed in concentration.

Once in the hallway, Maggie pulled out her cell phone,

planning to call Sam, but then she realized she didn't have his personal number in her phone. She had the station house, but she really didn't want to call there first.

She figured Sam would call her when he got the chance, and then she could save his number in her phone. The mere thought of having Sam's number in her phone gave her an odd little lift, which she immediately felt badly for, given that she was at the hospital with a friend whose husband was in emergency surgery while Diane, poor Diane, lay dead in the kitchen of the deli.

She scrolled through her contacts until she got to Ginger's number. The GBGs would want to know what was happening.

"Maggie," Ginger answered on the second ring. "So, how did your night end? Your place or Sam's?"

"Mine," Maggie said. "At the front door with a kiss, as all first dates should."

"Too many people in your house, huh?"

"You could say that," Maggie agreed. "Listen, I've got some bad news."

"What is it?" Ginger was instantly on high alert.

"Michael Claramotta is in emergency surgery for a head injury," she said. She heard Ginger gasp, but she went on before the questions could start. "I stopped by the deli this morning, but it was locked up. I was worried about Joanne, so I called her and she came over to check it out, because Michael was to have opened by then. Anyway"—Maggie paused to blow out a breath—"we found Michael unconscious and in a pool of his own blood."

"Oh no!" Ginger cried.

"It gets worse," Maggie said. "Diane Jenkins was there,

too, but she was dead. Ginger, it looks as if she was strangled with her apron strings."

"Ah!" Ginger let out a gasp of horror.

"Sam's over there now," Maggie said. "I'm with Joanne at the hospital. I need to call Laura at the shop, but I don't want to tell her about Diane over the phone. The two of them became friends over the past few days, and I know this is going to be a terrible shock."

"I'll go," Ginger offered. "You know how fast the gossip moves in this town. I'll go and tell her, and then we'll come to the hospital and sit with you and Joanne. I'll call Claire on my way."

"Thanks, Ginger," Maggie said. Ginger had been like a second mother to Laura. If Maggie couldn't be the one to tell Laura about Diane, it was best that it was going to come from Ginger.

"How are you holding up?" Ginger asked. Her voice was soft with caring, and Maggie knew that Ginger was remembering that night almost twenty years ago when she had stood by Maggie when Charlie had been in critical condition in this very hospital.

"I'm all right," Maggie said. "It helps to focus on Joanne and the baby."

"Have they said anything about Michael yet?"

"No, but I know Doc Franklin," Maggie said. "I could see on his face that it's bad."

She lowered her voice as if Joanne could hear her from down the hall.

"We'll get there as soon as we can," Ginger said. "Hang tough, sweetie."

"Will do," Maggie said.

She ended the call and made her way to the cafeteria. She fixed two coffees in to-go cups, high octane for her and decaf for Joanne. As she turned to leave the cafeteria, she heard her phone ring. She paused by a table to put the coffees down and dig her phone out of her pocket.

"Hello?" she answered.

"Maggie, it's Sam. How are you?" he asked.

"Waiting," Maggie said. "Michael is in surgery, so I'm doing the obligatory coffee run."

"How's Joanne?" he asked.

"Praying," Maggie said. "Or meditating, it was hard to tell which, although I imagine it was probably a little bit of both."

She glanced around the nearly empty cafeteria and realized that other than a few staff persons in scrubs and some in suits, the place was quiet. She figured the surge of visitors probably wouldn't start until later, and she was grateful for the calm.

"I've got the medical examiner and the crime-scene investigators here now," Sam said. "Once they're about finished, I'll meet you at the hospital."

"Okay," Maggie said. There was something in his tone that made her wary. "What aren't you telling me?"

Sam let out a sigh. "You're not going to like it."

"I figured that much," Maggie said. "So, let's just get it out."

"Diane was definitely strangled," Sam said. "And unless we find some evidence that someone else was in here with them, Michael is going to be a prime suspect."

Chapter 11

"But that's ridiculous," Maggie protested. "It could have been a robbery gone wrong or, well, something else."

Sam didn't say anything, and Maggie flashed onto the conversation she'd overheard at the ball between Michael and Diane. It had sounded like he was trying to break something off, something like a relationship. What if Diane had refused, and he'd strangled her? Well, then why would he have a head injury? Unless she'd managed to clock him on the head while he was strangling her, but then, where was the item used to knock him out? Maggie's mind raced through the possibilities.

"Let's hope the crime-scene investigators discover that it was a burglary," Sam said.

His voice was reluctant, and Maggie knew right away why. "Nothing was stolen, was it?"

"No," he said. "The office safe was untouched and the register was already loaded for the day, and it was untouched as well."

"It looks bad, doesn't it?" she asked.

"Yeah," he said. "I'm going to have to dig into the relationship between Michael and Diane, Maggie, and it may get messy."

Maggie sighed. She knew Sam was doing his job, and he was trying to prepare her for what was coming. She knew she should tell him what she had overheard. She opened her mouth to tell him, but then she thought of Joanne kissing her husband good-bye as he was wheeled off to surgery, and she couldn't do it. Not yet.

"I understand," she said.

"I'm sorry, Maggie." Sam sounded truly regretful, and Maggie felt a surge of guilt that she wasn't telling him what she knew.

She would wait, she decided, until after the crime-scene analysis was done. If it proved to be a burglary gone wrong, well, then the information she had was irrelevant and unnecessary.

"Me, too," she said.

Sam sighed, and Maggie knew he had no idea that she was apologizing to him and not just commiserating with him. She felt bad about it, and she really hoped that keeping what she knew to herself did not bite her on the butt later. She had a feeling that Sam in detective mode was not going to forgive her for holding information back from him.

She ended the call with a promise to let him know if there was a change in Michael's condition, and then she picked up the coffees and returned to her hard chair in the waiting room.

The Good Buy Girls filtered in and out of the waiting room all day long. They took turns sitting with Joanne, and Claire even dashed over from the library on her lunch hour to join the vigil.

Ginger had broken the news to Laura, who did not take it well at all. She came to the hospital with Ginger, and Maggie held her daughter while she cried over the loss of her new friend. When Claire left to go back to the library, Laura went with her. She wanted to be back in the shop. She said she needed to keep busy. Maggie couldn't blame her. Sitting in the tiny room was becoming excruciating.

The surgery took several hours, and when Joanne started to look pasty and likely to faint, Maggie forced some soup on her. She was sure Joanne was only eating for the baby, but that was fine.

When Doc Franklin appeared in the waiting room door, he looked haggard. He had been in the gallery that overlooked the operating room, keeping an eye on Michael for Joanne.

Joanne jumped up from her seat at the sight of him and immediately wobbled on her feet. Both Maggie and Ginger stood to support her.

"How is he, Doc?" she asked.

"He's stable," Doc said. "The surgeon will be in to talk to you shortly."

"Can I see him?" Joanne asked.

"In a bit," Doc said. He looked at Maggie and Ginger. "From recovery, he'll go to the ICU, where it will be family only."

"We are family," Ginger said in a growl.

Doc took in her fierce expression and he gave a faint smile. "Indeed you are."

"I'm afraid I have to get back to the office," he said. "Call me if you need me."

"We will," Maggie said. "Thanks, Doc, for everything."

"Yes," Joanne said. "Thank you."

Just then a nurse appeared at the door, "Mrs. Claramotta, if you'll follow me, you can visit your husband in recovery now."

Joanne hurried forward and Ginger went to follow, but the nurse blocked her. "Just his wife, please."

Ginger looked as if she'd argue, but Joanne gave her a small smile, and said, "It's okay. I'll be all right."

Ginger nodded, and Joanne hurried from the room with the nurse as if she was afraid the woman would change her mind.

"Okay, Doc," Ginger said. "Tell us what you know."

"He's no longer my patient," Doc said. "It's up to his surgeon, Dr. Graber, to tell Joanne what his status is."

Maggie nodded while Ginger's frown deepened.

"What I can tell you is that he's got his youth and good health going for him," Doc said. "But the blow to his head was severe. Now all we can do is wait until he wakes up to see what we're dealing with."

Maggie and Ginger exchanged glances, and Maggie knew Ginger was thinking the same thing that she was: This was going to be very hard on Joanne, and they were going to have to watch her round the clock to be sure she took care of herself and the baby.

When Joanne returned from the recovery room, she was visibly upset. Maggie and Ginger tried to talk her into going home to rest, but she was having none of it. Michael was being moved up to the ICU on the fifth floor, so she planned to move to the waiting room up there and visit Michael as much as she could.

Without having to discuss it, Maggie and Ginger made the move with her. When Joanne went into the ICU to see Michael settled, Ginger went to call Roger and her boys, and when she returned Maggie took a stroll down the hallway and called Laura to see how she was holding up.

"My Sister's Closet," Laura answered the shop phone. "May I help you?"

"Hi, sweetie," Maggie said. Her voice was gentle. She knew that Laura must have still been processing the news about Diane.

"Hi, Mom," Laura said. "How is Michael? Is he going to be all right? People have been calling the shop all afternoon."

"He's holding his own. He's out of surgery, but we have to wait until he wakes up to see how he is," Maggie said. She tried to keep her voice optimistic. "How are things at the shop?"

"Not terribly busy," Laura said. "We had a couple of returns and I made a few sales, but I have to say, my heart is really not in it. I can't stop thinking about Diane and I—"

Laura broke down and cried, and Maggie wished she could be there to wrap her in her arms and comfort her. She knew that Laura hadn't known Diane long, but still they'd seemed to hit if off so naturally. It had to be an awful shock.

"You know it's fine if you close the shop, honey," Maggie said.

"I know, but I'm afraid it will be worse if I go home and have nothing to do, and I don't want to freak Josh out by bursting into tears every few minutes," Laura said. She made a loud sniffle, and Maggie knew exactly what she meant. In times of disaster, Maggie liked to be busy, too.

"Have you talked to Sam? Does he know what happened?" Laura asked when she'd calmed down. "Were they robbed?"

"No one knows as yet," Maggie said. She knew it wasn't looking as if that were the case, and she knew her daughter would keep it to herself, but Maggie didn't even want to put it out there as yet.

"Well the local businesspeople are all getting very twitchy. In fact, Summer Phillips has hired Tyler Fawkes to patrol her shop," Laura said. "She even put him in a rent-a-cop uniform and everything."

Maggie rolled her eyes. Of course Summer had. If ever there was a person who brought attention to herself through someone else's tragedy, it was Summer.

"Tyler's even packing," Laura said.

"Packing what?"

"He's armed," Laura said.

"With a gun?" Maggie squawked.

"A Taser," Laura said.

"Oh, good grief," Maggie said. "I don't know who is dumber, Summer or Tyler. I swear they are a match made in heaven."

"Are you talking about us?" a voice asked from behind her.

Maggie turned to find Sam standing there, and she felt her face get hot. He thought she was talking about them? Then she saw the twinkle in his eye, and her insides turned to mush. How did he do that?

"Who's that?" Laura asked.

"Sam just arrived," Maggie said.

"Tell him I said hi," Laura said. "Call me if there's any change with Michael or any news."

"But—" Maggie began, but Laura had already ended the call.

"Laura says hi," she said.

Sam stepped closer and pulled her into a gentle hug. The solid feel of his arms around her made Maggie feel stronger, and she was grateful.

"I really like that girl," he said.

Maggie smiled against his shoulder before stepping back. "What's the good word?"

Sam pushed a strand of her long auburn hair back behind her ear. He looked pensive, and Maggie held her breath.

"No good word at the moment," he said. "As far as we can tell, the only two people in the deli this morning were Michael and Diane."

"But it's not conclusive yet, is it?"

"No, but it's not looking good," Sam said. "Maggie, I'm going to have to talk to Joanne."

Chapter 12

Sam looked so genuinely regretful that Maggie didn't have the heart to fight him on it, even though she wanted to.

"I'll be very tactful," he said.

Maggie nodded.

Together they walked back to the waiting room. When they entered, Joanne glanced up with hopeful eyes and Maggie knew she was hoping it was the doctor with good news.

"Hi, Joanne," Sam said as he took the seat on her right.

Ginger was on Joanne's left, and she gave Maggie a questioning glance. Maggie nodded, hoping Ginger would know that she meant they would talk later.

She took the seat across from the group and waited.

"Maggie tells me that Michael is holding his own," Sam said.

Joanne gave him a watery nod and fidgeted with the paper napkin in her hands. She'd been fretting it, twisting it tight with her fingers, but now she smoothed it out against her lap as if she could do the same with Michael's condition. She took a deep breath and met Sam's gaze with an intense look of her own.

"Who did this, Sam?" she asked. Her voice was stronger than Maggie expected, and she realized Joanne was angry. "Who would harm my Michael? And who would strangle that young woman?"

"Well, that's what I'm hoping you can help me with," Sam said. His voice was kind and gentle, and Maggie watched as Joanne's rage was quickly diverted into a cause.

"Absolutely," Joanne said. "I'll help in any way I can."

"What do you know about Diane Jenkins?" he asked.

"She's young," Joanne said. Realizing how it must have sounded, she quickly added, "I mean, she's in her early twenties. She's from Vermont or some state up north. She relocated to St. Stanley about two months ago just when Michael was looking for an assistant, you know, because of the baby. He wanted more flexibility. He wanted to hire someone with deli experience, and Diane answered the ad."

"Did either of you know her before that?" Sam asked.

Joanne narrowed her eyes. "What do you mean?"

Sam coughed, and said, "Was she referred to you by anyone? Had she worked for any business associates or family friends?"

"No." Joanne frowned and then paused. She looked pained when she added, "I guess I should say not that I know of. I've been so caught up with the baby, I, well, I haven't been paying much attention to the business. I should have been there this morning, but no, I was off choosing paint at the hardware store."

"Completely understandable," Ginger said, and patted Joanne's knee.

Joanne looked miserable. Maggie knew her well enough to know that she was thinking if she'd been more involved in the business that somehow this tragedy wouldn't have happened. But Maggie knew it probably would have, but it might have been even worse, in that Joanne and the baby could have been put in harm's way also. The thought made her shiver.

"Mrs. Claramotta." A doctor appeared in the door.

"Yes?" she asked. She rose from her seat, and Maggie could see the hope shining on her face.

"I'm sorry," Dr. Graber said. "There's been no change for better or for worse, but we're done with our examination if you'd like to sit with him now."

"I would. Thank you," she said. She looked at Sam and asked, "Do you need me for anything else?"

"No," he said. "I'll be in touch if there is anything to report."

"Thank you," she said, and she hurried after the doctor through the automatic door that led into the ICU.

"Maggie, you look done in," Ginger said. "Why don't you go home and have dinner. I'll stay until visiting hours are over and then take Joanne home. I've already convinced her that Michael would be unhappy if he knew she was planning to stay the night here."

"And she agreed?" Maggie asked.

"Baby on board is excellent leverage," Ginger said. "Claire is going to meet us at her place after the library closes and spend the night with her."

"Sounds good," Maggie said. "I want to make sure that Laura is all right."

They gave each other a quick hug, and Sam hugged Ginger, too.

"I'll give you a ride home," he said to Maggie. She gave him a considering look, and he asked, "What?"

"You look as bad as I feel," she said. "Take me home and I'll feed you some dinner."

Sam gave her a slow smile as they walked down the hall.

"I think I could get used to this," he said, and he pulled her close to his side as they made their way out of the hospital.

Maggie leaned into him, taking comfort from his strength. "I know what you mean."

Sam kissed her head before helping her into the car. They drove through town in companionable silence, which Maggie was pretty sure was a first for them. Usually, they were at odds over one thing or another.

She wondered how much of their squabbling had been because they'd still had a thing for each other and how much had been because they'd had different viewpoints. She had to admit that it felt good to let go of all her years of stored up anger with him. She wondered if he felt the same.

She thought he must, and then it hit her how fragile this new beginning was. She didn't want to be the one to damage the new trust they were trying out by withholding information, but she didn't want to wreak havoc with her friend's life either.

As Sam pulled up in front of her house, she knew she was going to have to tell him about the scene between Michael and Diane at the ball. She hated that she would be telling him something that she hadn't even told Joanne, but if it would help him find whoever had killed Diane, then she had to do it.

"What are you thinking about?" Sam asked as he opened her door for her.

Maggie met his gaze and was about to tell him, when the front door opened and Jake came out carrying Josh.

"Auntie Maggie!" Josh cried.

He reached out with his arms and Maggie took him from Jake. Holding Josh was the world's best medicine and, for the first time all day, Maggie felt just the tiniest bit better.

"Sorry," Jake said with a shrug. "Josh saw you through the window and wanted to say good night to you."

"Oh, good night, sweetie," Maggie said and kissed his soft, blond head.

"I didn't see you all day," Josh said. He leaned back and put both of his chubby hands on her cheeks. "I missed you."

Maggie felt a lump form in her throat. "I missed you, too."

"Come on, champ," Jake said. "It's time for bath and stories."

Maggie handed Josh back to his dad, and they all walked into the house together.

"Daddy's giving me a bath and telling me stories tonight," Josh announced. He wriggled with excitement.

Maggie looked at Jake's face and couldn't decide who looked happier about their time together, Josh or his dad.

She reached out and squeezed Jake's arm. "It's good to have you home."

"It's good to be here," he said.

"G'night, Josh," Sam said and held out his hand for a high five. Josh gave it a good whack, and Sam pretended to be hurt from the impact, which made Josh giggle.

Maggie and Sam waved as Jake headed down the hallway with his son. Together they made their way to the kitchen to find Laura finishing up the dishes while Sandy cleaned up the booster seat that Josh used to eat at the table.

"You know, I wonder how much actually gets into that boy's mouth given the amount he leaves behind on his seat," Sandy was saying as she brushed it off over the sink.

"Hi, Aunt Maggie, Sam," she said.

"Hi, Mom, Sam," Laura said as she turned from the sink. "I haven't packed up the leftovers yet. Are you hungry?"

"Oh, I'll get it," Maggie said. "I'll feel better if I have something to do."

Sitting all day in the waiting room had made her feel restless and edgy. She had kept longing for something—anything—to do, and had even wondered if the cleaning people would let her have a go with a mop for a while.

She took down two plates and started dishing out the leftover pot roast with potatoes and carrots for her and Sam.

"Is there any news?" Laura asked. Her voice was hesitant.

"No, not yet," Sam said. "I'm sorry."

"How's Joanne?" Sandy asked.

Maggie gave them an update on Joanne and Michael while she reheated dinner for her and Sam in the microwave. There wasn't much to tell, but she tried to put it in a positive light, as if by saying it that way she could make it so.

A splash and a squeal of delight sounded from down the hall in the bathroom.

"Excuse me," Sandy said. "I have a feeling I'm on cleanup duty—again."

They watched her go, and Maggie turned to Laura.

"Thank you for watching the shop today," she said.

"No problem," Laura said. Her eyes looked sad. "It was healthier than sitting home alone brooding. I still can't believe Diane's gone. I didn't know her for very long, but she seemed like she was beginning to come out of her shell, you know?"

"You knew her?" Sam glanced at Laura with interest.

"I was beginning to," Laura said. "She was very shy. It took a lot of persistence to get her to go out and do things."

Sam looked thoughtful. He asked Laura a few more questions, but she had no information. She and Diane had talked mostly about books, movies and clothes. She knew that Diane loved to read and was partial to old movies, but that was about it. She didn't know where exactly Diane was from or whether she had family nearby or anything.

"She never talked about herself," Laura said. She looked sheepish. "I think I did all of the talking for the two of us, which really makes me feel just awful."

Maggie rubbed her back. "It's okay, sweetie. I saw you make her laugh. She was as fond of you as you were of her."

Laura sniffed and pressed her lips together, obviously trying not to cry in front of Sam.

"If you think of anything else, anything at all, please tell me," Sam said. "We haven't been able to trace her family, and with Michael still unconscious, well, it's making contacting the next of kin pretty tough."

Maggie slid a plate in front of him at the counter and took the seat beside him.

"I will," Laura promised.

Feeling the need to change the conversation so that she could stomach her dinner, Maggie asked Laura about her day at the shop.

"You said earlier that we had some returns," Maggie said. "Which ones?"

"Well, Anna Kendrick brought back the Galliano, saying it didn't fit her," Laura said.

"But I saw her in it at the ball, and I know for a fact she had it altered to fit those boxy hips of hers," Maggie said. "We can't accept a return that's been tailored."

"Which is exactly what I told her," Laura said. "I told her it was a no-go unless she wanted to leave it with us as a consignment of which we'd take a cut of the resale."

"Good girl," Maggie said. "Well done."

"Thank you," Laura said, looking much less like she was going to cry. "I thought so."

"Any other messy returns?" Maggie asked.

"No, the other two were straightforward," Laura said. "One gown that hadn't been worn at all and a business suit for Mimi Carter. She was going to interview for a job in Richmond, but she changed her mind. She just didn't think she'd get along in the city very well."

"Which gown came back?"

"The Anne Barge," Laura said.

"Blake brought it back?" Maggie asked as she speared a chunk of meat on her fork. Sam was quietly chewing beside her, and she thought she could hear the gears in his head turning as he mulled over the events of the day.

Her chest tightened at the thought of the money they'd have to return on the Barge gown, but a part of her was thrilled to have the designer dress back. It was definitely going right back in the window for the holidays.

"Apparently, his fiancée did not want anything off the rack," Laura said in a mock snooty tone. "He was very apologetic about it."

"Some people just do not appreciate the value of resale,"

Maggie said with a shrug. "I'm sure whoever scores the dress will be thrilled."

"I know I would," Laura said.

Maggie smiled at her daughter. When Laura was growing up, Maggie had never been able to afford ballet lessons, manicures, pedicures and all of the other extras that most girls seemed to need to grow up these days. It had hurt Maggie deeply at the time to say no, but as a single mom with a mortgage to pay, she hadn't had any choice.

But now as she gazed at her kind, funny, brilliant and beautiful daughter, and saw a young woman who had worked her butt off to earn a scholarship to the university of her choice and who took nothing for granted; maybe all of the noes had been a good thing.

"I love you, baby," she said.

Laura grinned, and said, "I love you, too, Mom."

Sam glanced between them and smiled as if he, too, understood the genuine affection and respect that Maggie and Laura shared.

"Good pot roast," he said.

"I'll tell Sandy you said so," Laura offered. "And on that note, I'm going to bed. I'm just . . ."

Her voice trailed off, and Maggie knew exactly what she meant. They were all overwhelmed by what had happened.

"Call me if you need me," Maggie said. "My tuck-in service never expires."

Laura laughed. "Thanks, Mom. Good night."

Sam got up from his chair and began to clean his dishes in the sink, adding them to the dishwasher, which had yet to be run.

"Have I mentioned how much I like that kid?" he asked.

"Yes," Maggie said. "But a proud mom never tires of hearing it."

He reached across the counter and took her empty plate. "Seconds?" he asked.

"No thanks." Maggie shook her head. It had taken all she had just to finish that serving, which hadn't been much.

Sam cleaned her plate and put it in the dishwasher, too.

"You really did a great job in raising her," he said. "She's a woman of substance."

"Oh, I like that," Maggie said.

Sam came around the counter and pulled her to her feet.

"She takes after her mother," he said.

Maggie felt her face grow warm at the compliment.

"Come on, let's sit awhile before I have to go back to the station," Sam said.

He held her hand as they made their way to the sunporch. They sat on a cushy love seat, and Sam put his arm around the back of the small couch and pulled Maggie close.

She rested her head on his shoulder and felt comforted. It had been such a scary day. A part of her just wanted to melt into Sam and let him be her strength but, of course, she couldn't. Instead, she needed to tell him what she knew.

"Sam," she said. "I probably should have told you this before, but I hope you'll understand why I didn't."

"What is it?" he asked.

"I think I might know something," she said. "Something about Michael and Diane."

Chapter 13

Sam's hand had been running up and down her arm. It stilled when she spoke, as if he was bracing himself for what she might say.

"What's that?" he asked. His voice was decidedly neutral.

"I saw them at the ball," she said. She turned to look at him and was distracted by how near his face was to hers and by what a pure shade of blue his eyes were. She turned away to keep herself focused.

Sam said nothing, seemingly content to let Maggie tell him what she'd seen in her own time.

"After we welcomed Jake back, I was a soggy mess," she said. "So I went in search of a mirror, but someone was in the bathroom nearest the ballroom. I was working my way down the hall, looking for another, when I accidentally found myself in a large pantry."

She cleared her throat. She didn't want this to sound worse than it was, but in hindsight, it looked pretty bad.

"Michael and Diane were in there, and they were having an argument—no, that's not the right word. It was a discussion. Yes, definitely a discussion."

"What sort of discussion?" Sam's hand started moving up and down her arm again.

Maggie cleared her throat in a blatant stall tactic. She wanted to be sure she worded this just right.

"Michael was saying something about how 'this can't go on' and he had to 'think about Joanne and the baby.'" Maggie blew out a breath and twisted her fingers in her lap.

Sam's hand tightened on her arm and pulled her close. He kissed the top of her head as if he knew she needed comforting. His voice was cautious when he said, "It sounds like he was breaking off a relationship."

"Yeah," Maggie said. "I didn't want Joanne to know. It was so hard for her to get pregnant, and she's not that far along. I would hate for her to be hit with more stress than she's already under. Is there any way to keep it from her?"

Sam sighed. "I'm sorry, Maggie, but I don't see how."

"Damn," Maggie muttered.

"Thank you for telling me," he said.

"You sound surprised," she said.

"I am," he admitted. "You haven't been exactly forthcoming with me in the past."

Maggie turned to meet his gaze. "I know, but things are different now. I trust you."

Sam leaned close and rested his forehead against hers, and whispered, "Thank you."

Maggie felt something change between them. It was subtle, like the breeze shifting in a new direction.

"In the interest of full disclosure, I have some information, too," he said. "We searched Michael's office to find Diane's personnel file so we could inform her next of kin. There wasn't one."

"I don't understand," Maggie said.

"There was no record of her in any of Michael's files," he said. "Or on his computer."

"That's impossible," Maggie said. "He'd have to have tax forms, payroll sheets, that sort of stuff."

Sam shook his head. "It's as if she didn't even exist."

"Do you think he was paying her under the table?" Maggie asked.

"He'd have had to," Sam said. "But why?"

Neither of them spoke. Maggie didn't like where her thoughts were going, and she suspected Sam was thinking the same thing.

"The obvious reason is that Michael was having an affair with Diane and didn't want to leave any sort of paper trail." There. She'd said it, and she felt awful about it.

"I thought that, too," he said. "But then, I wonder."

"What?"

"Well, wouldn't Joanne be more suspicious if she found no file on her husband's new hire than if it was above board and perfectly normal?"

"I see what you mean," Maggie said. "The fact that there is no paper trail is way more suspicious than if he'd treated her like a normal employee, so why would he do that? Michael is not that stupid."

"Exactly," Sam said.

"You know, they have an office in their house," Maggie said. "Maybe he keeps the personnel files there."

"The rest of the staff files are at the deli," Sam said. "Why wouldn't hers be?"

"Well, she's new, so maybe he was keeping it at home while she was on probation?" Maggie asked. "Or maybe Joanne took it home to look it over?"

"Why would she do that?"

Maggie sighed. "Joanne was just the teensiest bit concerned about Michael's new hire."

Sam turned and faced her. "Define concerned."

Maggie hated this. She hated that her new relationship with Sam required her to share the angst of a friend.

"She was jealous, which is perfectly normal in a pregnant woman," she rushed to assure him. "I mean, you're hormonal and overtired, you feel huge and you're not in control of your body anymore. Of course you feel threatened if your husband suddenly hires some cute young thing."

"Are you speaking from experience?" Sam asked.

"A bit," Maggie said.

His gaze was warm. "I bet you were adorable when you were pregnant."

"I was fat," Maggie said. "I looked like I'd swallowed a watermelon. There was nothing cute about it."

Sam smiled at her, clearly not appreciating how unattractive and emotionally difficult she had been with a bun in her oven.

"You said you called Joanne when you found the deli locked," Sam said.

"I did," Maggie said. "She was at the hardware store, looking at paint."

Sam nodded.

"Wait. You don't think Joanne—" she began, but he shook his head.

"No, I know she was shopping at the time of the murder. Even Jerry Paulson, who owns the hardware store, placed her there."

The fact that he had corroborated Joanne's story caused Maggie to feel a flash of irritation.

"So, you checked her out?" she asked.

"Only to verify what she told me in the ICU waiting room today—to rule her out," he said. "I think she felt guilty that she wasn't in the deli, but I know Michael would have wanted her and the baby safely away from whatever happened."

"Agreed," Maggie said. "What happens next?"

"We keep trying to find Diane's next of kin, we wait for Michael to wake up and we keep searching for clues as to what actually happened at the deli," he said.

"Is there anything I can do to help?" she asked.

"I'd ask you to stay away from it, but I'm guessing that's not going to happen."

"Yeah, probably not," she said. "They're my friends."

"I know." He pulled her close into a half hug. "Your loyalty is one of the things I—like most about you."

Maggie noticed the tiny hesitation, and she was grateful for it. She didn't think either of them were ready to go further than *like* no matter what they were feeling on the inside.

"I like the same thing about you," she said. And then she kissed him.

It was a long while later before Sam took his leave. Maggie waved from the front door as he backed his car up and drove away. She was torn between feeling miserable for her friend and happy for herself. She hoped Joanne was doing all right. And she really hoped Michael woke up soon so that they would have some answers.

She shut off the lights in the living room as she made her way to her bedroom. She paused beside a picture of Charlie holding Laura when she had just been learning how to walk.

She traced his smile with her finger. She still missed him. Having Sam back in her life didn't change that, but somehow she felt like Charlie would approve of Sam. He was a lawman like Charlie had been, and he was a good person. She knew that more than anything would have satisfied Charlie. She kissed the tip of her finger and tapped Charlie's nose.

"Good night," she said. She switched out the light and headed off to bed.

Maggie woke up by rolling onto a toy train that whistled when she crushed it with her hip. The piercing sound made her snap awake and sit straight up as she tried to figure out what was making that awful racket.

The tiny towhead who'd climbed into bed beside her sometime in the night slept on, blissfully unaware of the shrill noise his train was making. Maggie fumbled in the sheets until she found the train and switched it off.

She flopped back against her pillows. She glanced at her alarm clock. It was early, but she knew she wouldn't be able to get back to sleep.

She slipped out of bed, careful not to wake Josh, and

headed to the kitchen to make coffee and a nice coffee cake. She had a feeling the grown-ups were all going to need a little something extra to get going today. Besides, she knew apple streusel was Laura's favorite and, having lost her new friend in such a grisly way yesterday, the poor girl needed something to comfort her.

Maggie was showered and dressed, reading the paper and sipping her coffee while the coffee cake baked, when Laura and Sandy stumbled into the kitchen.

"Morning, Mom," Laura said while she poured herself a steaming mug. Then she sniffed the air. "Is that an apple streusel coffee cake?"

"Yes, it is."

"Aw, thanks, Mom." Laura circled the counter and hugged her. "So, I never heard Sam leave last night."

"Hmm, I didn't either," Sandy chimed in.

To Maggie's chagrin, she felt her face grow warm with embarrassment. "He left sometime around eleven, I believe."

"Oh, well, that's disappointing," Laura said.

Sandy laughed, and Maggie huffed, "We've only just started dating. Don't rush us."

"Yes, but you dated in high school," Laura said. "That should move things along quicker, shouldn't it?"

"No," Maggie said. "If anything, we're more cautious. We don't want to mess it up this time."

"You won't," Sandy said. "When Sam looks at you, it's like—"

"How Jake looks at you," Laura interrupted. "As if you're the only woman on Earth. I hope I find that someday."

"You will," Maggie and Sandy said together, and then they laughed.

As Maggie sliced and served coffee cake, the conversation turned back to Michael and Joanne. Maggie didn't tell them what she and Sam had discussed.

It felt like it would be a betrayal of Joanne's friendship to discuss the possibility that Michael was involved with Diane. Especially since Maggie didn't believe it. She didn't care what she'd overheard or how bad it had looked, Michael and Joanne were the real deal. She just couldn't imagine one without the other, and she just couldn't believe that Michael had stepped out on Joanne, especially when she was expecting their first child.

She wondered if it was too early to call Sam to find out if they'd made any progress in locating Diane's family. She glanced at the clock. It was just after eight. She had a feeling that Joanne was already at the hospital.

Maggie fished her cell phone out of her purse. She scanned through her messages. Sure enough, there was a text message from Claire from an hour earlier that she and Joanne were headed back to the hospital. It had been sent to both Maggie and Ginger. She texted back that she was on her way and put her phone back in her purse.

"I'm going to go to the hospital to check on Michael before I go to the shop," Maggie said.

"I'll come with you," Laura said.

"Are you sure?" Maggie asked.

"Yes, that way if Joanne needs you, I can go open the shop for you," she said. "I was thinking I'd put the Barge gown back in—"

"The front window," Maggie said with her. "I was thinking the same thing."

They smiled at each other in perfect understanding.

"I'll just go and get dressed," Laura said.

She passed Jake on her way as he joined Sandy and Maggie in the kitchen. Jake was still in his flannel pajama bottoms and T-shirt. He planted a kiss on Sandy's head as he passed her to get to the coffeepot.

"Good morning, ladies," he said.

"Mornin'," they answered.

"How did you sleep, Jake?" Maggie asked.

He and Sandy exchanged a quick glance, and Maggie saw Sandy turn a pretty shade of pink before she turned away to cut Jake a piece of the coffee cake.

"Really well," Jake said with a grin. He took a sip of his coffee, and said, "Maggie, I can't thank you enough for letting Sandy and Josh live with you for the past few years. It would have been hard for Sandy to leave school to go live with her mother in Florida and, well, it gave me real peace of mind to know that she and Josh were being looked after by you."

"We're family," Maggie said. "That's what family does. Besides, it's been a pleasure watching Josh grow. He is very dear to me."

Sandy and Jake exchanged another look, but this time it was one of concern. Maggie knew what was coming. She had known since Jake had returned. She suspected that they were worried about how she would take it, and that made them both even more precious to her.

"So when are you three moving out?" she asked.

Jake looked at her in surprise.

"What?" she asked. "Did you really think I thought you'd all live here with me indefinitely?"

"Well, no, but we didn't want to make you sad around the holidays," Sandy said.

"Now, do not worry about me," Maggie said. "You two have had to put your life together on hold while Jake was deployed, but he's home now, and I know you're eager to be a family. I am the default babysitter for Josh, however. That is not negotiable."

Sandy grinned and circled the counter to give Maggie a fierce hug. "Thanks, Aunt Maggie."

Maggie felt her throat get tight. She loved her niece like a daughter. And as brave a face as she put on, it still hurt to let her go.

"I've got my eye on a small fixer-upper just around the corner," Jake said. He was watching her as if he knew she was acting stronger than she was actually feeling. She appreciated that he was trying to make it easier for her.

"Really?" Maggie asked. "Which one?"

"It's over on Elm Street. It's the pale blue house with white trim, but it looks like the front porch is rotted out," he said.

"Oh, that's the old Kerrigan house," Maggie said. "They were such a nice family."

"We're going to the bank today to see if we can get preapproved to make an offer," Sandy said.

"If you need anything—a signature, a pint of blood, my left foot," Maggie said, "you ask me."

"I'm hoping the left foot is not necessary," Jake said with a laugh. "But we'll let you know about the pint of blood."

Maggie grinned at him.

Laura arrived back in the kitchen, and asked, "Are you ready?"

Maggie's phone chimed, and she grabbed it back out of her purse. It was Sam.

"Hello," she answered.

"Morning, Maggie," he said.

She felt her spirits lift at the sound of his voice.

"I was just headed over to the hospital to check on Joanne," she said. "Is there any news I can bring her?"

Sam heaved a sigh that sounded as if it came all the way up from his feet, and Maggie knew that whatever it was, it was bad.

Chapter 14

"Oh no. What is it?" she asked.

"Can't talk about it on the cell," he said. "I'll meet you at the hospital in ten minutes?"

"I'm on my way," Maggie said. She ended the call and looked over at Laura. "Sam has some sort of news. Let's fly."

"Be careful," Jake said.

"I will," Maggie said.

"Give Joanne my best," Sandy called after her.

"Will do," Maggie said as she led the way out to her Volvo station wagon.

Laura climbed into the passenger seat and glanced at her mother. "I was going to say we should hit the Daily Grind for coffee on the way, but I'm guessing it's straight to the hospital for us."

"Sorry, honey, but it sounds like Sam has information," Maggie said. "And it doesn't sound good."

"So, no suspects yet?"

Maggie pressed her lips together. What was she supposed to say? That the most likely suspect was her friend's husband, who was lying in a coma?

"No, not yet," she said.

They were silent for the rest of the ride. When they got to the waiting room for the ICU, they found Ginger sitting by herself.

"Joanne is in with Michael," she said. "They said she could visit for fifteen minutes before the doctors came to check him over."

"How is she holding up?" Maggie asked.

"She's made of tough stuff," Ginger said. "Even with the hormone overload she's got going on, she's been doing really well."

Maggie nodded. "I can wait for her if you need to get back to work."

"I don't have a client scheduled until ten," Ginger said. "I stayed up late last night, working on his file so I could relieve Claire this morning so she could get to the library."

"That was really good of you," Maggie said.

"No more than you," Ginger said. "This is why we run our own businesses. Flexibility."

"I'll watch the shop today, Mom," Laura said. "It was good to be busy yesterday, and Mrs. Swopes dropped off a big box of coats that have to be gone through. I think some of them will need to be dry-cleaned, as they smell like her cedar-lined closet, but otherwise they looked to be in great shape."

"I don't want to take up all of your free time with the shop," Maggie said. "Maybe it would be better for you to be visiting with your friends, you know, to get your mind off things."

"Max and Bianca are coming by the shop for lunch," Laura said. "And Aaron said he'd pop in after his shift at the health-food store. Maybe I'm suspicious, but I'm getting the feeling that people are afraid to leave me alone."

"Aaron mentioned that he was worried about you," Ginger said. "He knew you were trying to help Diane adjust to the town and make some friends. He said she was a very nice girl."

"She really was," Laura said. She looked sad and then glanced at the doors to the ICU, which were closed, and asked, "How about I go get us all some coffee?"

"That'd be nice," Maggie said. "Thanks."

"Yes. Thank you," Ginger said.

Both women dug into their purses to give Laura some money, but she waved them off.

"Please," she said. "It's the least I can do."

Maggie watched Laura walk away and looked at her oldest friend.

"Should I go after her?" she asked. "I'm having a hard time with the fact that my baby is a grown woman."

"I think she's all right," Ginger said. "But I know what you mean. I feel as if I blinked, and suddenly all four of my boys were taller than me."

Sam came into the room just then. He was in uniform, the standard dark slacks and a long-sleeve white dress shirt and tie with his badge clipped on the left front pocket. His dark blue jacket was unzipped, as if he'd shrugged it on in a hurry.

"Hi, Maggie, Ginger," he said.

He crossed the room toward them just as the ICU doors swung open and Joanne came out, looking pale and drained. She joined them in the corner and slumped into a chair. Maggie and Ginger began to fuss over her.

"Are you all right?"

"How's Michael?"

"Can we get you anything?"

"I'm fine." Joanne said. Clearly, it was a lie. "Michael's the same. He hasn't woken up. No, there's nothing I need. But thanks."

"Have you eaten this morning?" Maggie asked.

"Claire made pancakes," Joanne said. They looked at her, and she added, "Yes, I ate some. You can call her and check."

She glanced past Maggie and Ginger at Sam. She didn't say anything, but she looked at him questioningly.

"No, there's no news on my end either," he said.

"Meaning there are no suspects in custody as yet?" Joanne clarified.

"Not yet," Sam confirmed.

The waiting room door opened, and Alice Franklin, Doc Franklin's wife, entered the room. She scanned the chairs until she saw Joanne, and she hurried right over.

"Joanne, I heard about what happened," she said. She sat down next to Joanne and gave her a bracing half hug. "If there is anything you need, please let me know. I've already got a group organizing meals to be delivered to your house, and when Michael is released, we'll make sure that whatever medical equipment you need will be waiting for you."

Joanne gave her a wan smile. "Thanks, Alice. I really appreciate it."

Maggie wasn't surprised to see Alice here, as she was on

the hospital board as well as several other civic-minded committees. Alice was a very active member of the St. Stanley community, and Maggie imagined that even while Doc and Alice were estranged Alice was still a powerhouse of good deeds and acts of kindness.

The waiting room doors opened again, and Doc Franklin entered the waiting room with Laura. He held the door for her while she carried a tray full of coffees.

There was a beat of silence while everyone in the room glanced between Doc and Alice and then studiously looked anywhere but at the two of them. Awkward.

"I'm sorry, Sam, Mrs. Franklin," Laura said. "I'd have brought you both coffees as well, if I'd known you were here."

"That's fine, dear," Alice said. "I was just leaving."

She gave Joanne's shoulder one more squeeze and then rose from her seat, nodding at the rest of them while she flagrantly ignored her husband. When the door shut behind her, Maggie glanced quickly at Doc, who was looking at the door through which his wife had disappeared with a look of consternation.

"And don't worry about me," Sam said to Laura. "Deputy Wilson makes the station house coffee with more rev in its engine than a V-8. I'll be good until mid-afternoon."

"Oh, I'll have to try it sometime," Laura said, obviously trying to lighten the mood of the room as she handed out coffees to Joanne, Ginger and Maggie.

"I'm going to go and consult with Michael's doctor," Dr. Franklin said when he finally turned away from the door. "I'll see if I can pry any information out of him."

"Oh, thank you, Doc," Joanne said.

Ginger and Laura took seats on either side of Joanne.

Maggie glanced at Sam. She remembered that he had something to tell her. She raised her eyebrows at him in a silent question, and he gave her a slight nod.

"I'm going to get back to the station," he said. "Joanne, please let me know if you need anything or if there is any change in Michael's condition."

"I will," Joanne said. "Thanks for checking in, Sam."

Sam glanced back at Maggie. "Walk me out?"

"Sure. I'll be right back," she said to the others.

Maggie sipped her coffee as they rode the elevator down to the lobby. Sam was tense. She could feel stress coming off him in waves. She had a feeling that whatever he wanted to tell her was not going to be pleasant.

Once they reached the main lobby of the hospital, Sam took her aside to a deserted sitting area.

"What is it, Sam?" she asked. "The suspense is killing me."

He looked at her, and she sighed. "Sorry. Bad choice of words."

"It's okay," he said. They sat side by side on a small couch. Sam ran a hand through his hair as if trying to figure out how to tell her what he had to say. Maggie took another sip of coffee and waited.

"I've been reconstructing Diane's life in St. Stanley. There are some interesting things about it, like she didn't have a car," Sam said. "Now, she lived in an apartment in the center of town, so walking to the deli was no big deal for her."

He paused, and Maggie said nothing.

"According to Conner Bishop, who's worked for Michael

for almost five years, Michael let Diane use the deli's car," he said. "She did some deliveries for him, and she used it a few times for personal errands."

"Okay," Maggie asked. "I'm not sure why this is important. Not everyone owns a car."

"True," Sam said. "But Diane didn't have a license on file with the deli, which makes it surprising to me that Michael would let her use the deli's car. If she had gotten into an accident, it could have been a disaster. Conner verified that the rest of the deli staff had to have their license on file with Michael before they could use the van. Then again, it's not a big surprise that there is no license on file for Diane, given that she doesn't have a personnel file at all."

"Okay, so other than another lack of information, what else did you find?" Maggie asked.

Sam met her gaze with a steady one of his own.

"We searched Diane's apartment. There was nothing there—no photos, no letters, no computer, no telephone, no bills or mail of any kind. Her landlord, Mrs. Denton, said she paid her rent in cash. And Mrs. Denton only rented to Diane because Michael vouched for her."

"Weird," Maggie said.

"It gets weirder. I searched the deli's van on the off chance that Diane had left any documentation in there. I thought maybe she kept her license in the glove box or something."

Maggie could hear the resigned note in his voice. This was it. He had found something.

"What did you find?" she asked.

"An envelope," he said and then paused. He let out a long, slow breath. "It was an envelope full of pictures of Diane."

"I don't understand," Maggie said. Then her mouth formed a little O. "They aren't dirty pictures, are they?"

Sam shook his head. "No, but they are disturbing. They are all close-ups, but the feeling you get when you look at them is that Diane had no idea someone was taking her picture. I think whoever took them was using a high-powered zoom lens. The shots are of her in the deli, walking through town, having coffee at the Daily Grind and in her apartment. Whoever took the photos was cataloging her every second of every day as if they were completely obsessed with her."

"What are you saying?" Maggie asked. Her voice was tight. She really didn't like where this conversation was going.

"The van is Michael's," Sam said. "It is registered to him as a commercial vehicle for when the deli does catering."

"I know that," Maggie snapped. She immediately felt bad about it, but she wanted Sam to come out and say what he was thinking. "I want you to tell me what you think of what you've found, and I want to know what you're going to do about it."

"I think someone was stalking Diane," Sam said. "And I think, given the conversation that you overheard between her and Michael, that it definitely had something to do with him."

"No!" Maggie argued. "That doesn't make any sense. If Michael was obsessed with her and stalking her, he wouldn't have been trying to break up with her."

"Agreed," Sam said. "But maybe it wasn't Michael who was stalking her, maybe it was a jealous spouse."

"Joanne?" she scoffed.

Sam shrugged.

"That's ridiculous!" Maggie snapped. "It's stupid, preposterous and just dumb. Joanne would never harm anyone—ever."

"I'm sorry, Maggie, but I'm going to have to bring Joanne in and question her about Michael and Diane's relationship, and I'm going to have to show her the pictures."

Chapter 15

"But you can't!" Maggie protested. "She's so fragile right now. If Michael was having an affair, it will kill her. You have to think about the baby."

"I am truly sorry if this causes Joanne any distress," he said. "But—"

"No, there are no *but*s," she said as she leapt to her feet. "You can't do this to her when her husband is lying in a coma and might never wake up. What if the last thing she ever knows about him is that he had an affair?"

"Maggie, make no mistake: I hate this. But I have a young woman who will never see another birthday, never get married and never have a child of her own, and why? Because someone murdered her, and it is my job to figure out who."

He stood, too, and now they were facing each other.

"And you really think that someone is Joanne?"

"Honestly?" he asked. "No. Joanne was at the hardware store just like she said and that looks good for her and statistically speaking only three percent of all murders committed against men are carried out by a wife or girlfriend, and the stats are even lower for female-on-female murder. But this isn't about what I think. I have to look at the facts, Maggie. And when I do look at them, what choice do I have?"

"You have a choice to wait," she said. "To not terrorize a pregnant woman who is already scared out of her mind."

"Well, gee, when you put it like that," he growled.

"How can I not?" she asked. "There's a family at stake here."

"And what about Diane?" Sam asked. "Doesn't she matter?"

"Of course she does," Maggie said. She felt guilt twist her insides as she thought of the timid young woman. "I never said that she didn't."

"Look," Sam said. "Joanne has all of you. No matter what we find out, she isn't alone. Diane has no one."

Maggie hung her head. She knew he was right, but she knew that she was right, too. There was a family involved here, and until the truth was absolute, she didn't think they should be put at risk.

"I have to find out what happened to Diane, and I'm sorry if it upsets Joanne, I really am, but this is my job and I have to do it."

"You won't bend on this?" she asked.

"I can't," he said.

"Well, I guess there's nothing more to say."

They stared at each other, and Maggie felt as if, despite every step forward they had taken, they'd just leapt back a mile.

"I guess not," he agreed.

"Are you going to question her now?" she asked. She could hear that her voice was hostile, but she didn't know how to temper it.

"No, it'll be a bit later," he said. "After I've met with the coroner to go over his report."

"Will you make sure she has someone there for her when you do it?"

"Really?" he asked. "You have to ask me that?"

Maggie crossed her arms over her chest and glared.

"Yes, I'll make sure *Ginger* is there," he said.

"Fine," she said. Why that made her mad, she had no idea, but all of a sudden they might as well have been in grammar school again, with him taunting her and her rising to the bait every time. "You do that."

Maggie spun on her heel and began to stalk back to the waiting room to be with her friends.

"Maggie, wait!" Sam said.

She almost didn't turn around, but she wasn't ready to let go of all that had changed between them. She stopped, lowered her head and heaved a breath. When she turned around, Sam was coming toward her with the most intense look on his face that she had ever seen. It narrowed the world into just the two of them and made her breath catch.

He cupped her face, and then he kissed her. Maggie was so surprised, she couldn't stop her response and her arms were around his neck and pulling him closer even as she knew that she was still mad at him.

When they broke apart, he rested his forehead against hers. They were both breathing heavily.

"I don't want this to come between us," he said.

"I don't either," she said. "But I don't see how it can't."

Sam hugged her. "We're better than this. We'll just keep talking, and we'll work through it. I'll do everything I can to keep from traumatizing Joanne. I promise."

Maggie nodded. She knew Sam would try, but the truth was, she was terrified by what he had discovered. She didn't even want to consider the possibility that what Sam had told her was true.

But she couldn't shake off Joanne's jealousy of Diane and what she had seen between Michael and Diane at the ball. And now it appeared that Diane had virtually no history, and there were pictures of her in Michael's van, pictures taken by someone who had been stalking her. It was too much. Maggie didn't even know how she was going to go back upstairs and face Joanne like everything was normal.

"All right," she said, and she hugged him once more. She could feel that things were still awkward between them, but maybe only time could fix that. "Let's try."

"How about dinner tonight, say seven o'clock?" he asked as he stepped back.

"Okay," she said.

She turned to go back to the waiting room, giving Sam a quick wave as the elevator doors closed behind her.

As soon as she stepped off the elevator on five, she fished her phone out of her purse. She opened her contacts and fired a quick text to Claire. They needed to have an emergency meeting of the GBGs as soon as possible.

She knew Claire would come back to the hospital on her lunch hour, and that would give them a chance to strategize. She had no doubt that Sam wouldn't be happy with her for what he was sure to think of as her meddling, but it couldn't be helped. These were her friends, and she could no more sit by and watch their world torn apart than she could pass up a two-for-one sale.

It was just minutes after one o'clock when Claire raced into the waiting room. She was wearing a navy pencil skirt with a pretty paisley blouse and matching navy pumps. Her blonde bob was windswept and her dark rectangular glasses were perched on her nose as if she was ready for any reference question that could be fired at her.

Ginger and Maggie were sitting in the corner. Joanne had gone into the ICU to sit with Michael, and Laura had left a while ago to go tend the shop. It was the perfect time for a meeting.

"How is Michael?" Claire asked as she hugged both Ginger and Maggie. "And Joanne?"

"No change with Michael," Ginger said.

"Joanne is holding up very well, all things considered," Maggie said.

Claire slipped into an available chair. "So, what can we do to help?"

Maggie had been thinking over what she could and couldn't tell the others. She didn't want to compromise Sam's investigation, but she had to tell them something so that they would understand what they were dealing with and why it was so critical that they find out more about Diane.

"Sam has been having a very hard time trying to track down Diane's next of kin," she said.

Ginger and Claire gave her curious looks, and Maggie explained that there was no file for her in the deli and that Sam had been unable to find any link to her past in her apartment.

"That's weird, isn't it?" Claire asked.

"Maybe it's just an oversight," Ginger offered, although it didn't sound as if she believed it. Being a CPA, she wasn't big on oversights when it came to paperwork.

"I want to look at her apartment," Maggie said.

"Why?" Ginger asked.

"Because maybe we can find something that Sam missed," Maggie said.

"Yeah, because a thrift-store owner, a librarian and a CPA are so much better at investigating than one of Richmond's former finest?" Ginger asked.

"Don't be a doubter," Maggie said.

"And if Sam finds out we're doing this?" Claire asked.

"I don't see any reason why he should," Maggie said.

"We live in a town the size of Q-tip," Ginger said. "Of course he's going to find out."

"Find out what?" Joanne asked.

The three women were startled to discover that Joanne had come into the room without them noticing.

"Um . . . uh," Maggie stammered, stalling for time.

"Sam will find out that we're trying to learn what happened to Diane and Michael," Claire said.

Joanne stared at each of them in turn. "Okay, now what aren't you telling me?"

"Whatever do you mean?" Ginger asked in her most innocent tone of voice.

"Please," Joanne said. "You three have guilt with a capital *G* imbedded on all of your foreheads. Why do you think you need to help find out what happened to Diane and Michael? What's going on?"

She crossed her arms over her chest and glared. Maggie looked at Ginger who looked at Claire who looked back at Maggie. It was clear that the other two did not want to take charge of this conversation.

"We were thinking we should find out more about Diane's past," Maggie said. There. That was nice and vague and didn't give anything away.

"Why?" Joanne asked. "Isn't that Sam's job?"

"It is," Maggie agreed.

"But we think we might be able to help," Ginger said. "Being the enterprising type of women that we are."

Joanne gave them a small smile, and her stiff posture relaxed. "I love that about you all. Is there anything I can do to pitch in?"

"You just watch over Michael," Claire said. "We'll take care of the rest."

"Thank you," Joanne said as she slumped into an empty seat and they all rallied around her. Claire went to the cafeteria to bring her lunch while Ginger put an arm around her and Maggie held her hand.

Maggie noticed that while Joanne sat, her slowly emerging tummy looked bigger than before, and a fierce protectiveness filled Maggie. They would help Joanne find out what happened at the deli, and her baby would not grow up like Laura had, without her father.

"So, where do we start?" Claire asked. She was dressed head to toe in unrelieved black, just like Ginger and Maggie.

"That depends—where would you hide any personal documents that you didn't want found?" Ginger asked.

They were standing in Diane's apartment. It was a one-bedroom that was sparsely decorated with just the essentials. A bed and dresser were in the bedroom along with a small couch and television, and a café table and two chairs decorated the main room. The closet in the bedroom had minimal clothes and shoes. The kitchen had just enough cookware and dishware for one person.

Maggie knew that Sam had already been here. There was no computer or telephone to be found, and she wondered if Diane had even owned either of those.

She had to remember to ask Laura if Diane had had a cell phone. She didn't imagine that Laura had always called the deli to get in touch with Diane, but maybe she had.

Maggie glanced around the room as she considered Ginger's question.

"Maybe her personal papers were taped to the bottom of a dresser drawer," she said.

"You've watched way too many episodes of *Sherlock*," Claire said even as she went to the bedroom to start checking the bottoms of the dresser drawers.

Maggie spied a canister set on the counter and went to inspect that, while Ginger checked the kitchen cupboards and drawers for any clues. They continued on through the apartment, looking for any possible hidey-hole for personal documents or photos. There was nothing.

Finally, they sat in the middle of the living room floor, defeated.

"It's as impersonal as a motel room," Claire said. "There's clothes and food and nothing else."

"I have a really bad feeling about this," Ginger said.

"It's like she didn't want to leave a hair or even a finger-print behind," Maggie said.

"It's strange," Ginger agreed. "Most people can't get enough attention. Look at how lame television has become, with every reality-star loser trying to spin their fifteen min-utes of stupid into a career."

They all shuddered.

"There's only one reason I can think of that her place would be this barren," Claire said. "She was in hiding. She didn't want to be found."

Ginger and Maggie both studied Claire. A few months ago, she had been someone who didn't want to be found. She'd come to St. Stanley with a new identity, hoping to start over, but her past had found her. Had the same thing hap-pened to Diane?

"No wonder Sam is so frustrated," Maggie said.

Ginger glanced at her cell phone. "Speaking of Sam, don't you two have a date in half an hour?"

Ginger held up the phone so Maggie could see the time. Ginger was right. She had thirty minutes to get home and get ready.

"Yikes!" She bolted up from her seat. "Thank Mrs. Den-ton for me, will you?"

Mrs. Denton was one of Ginger's clients, and she had agreed to let them look at the apartment in return for a discount on her next tax preparation.

"Yes, now go!" Ginger promised. "I'll be at Joanne's tonight if you need to call for advice or anything."

Maggie rolled her eyes at her friend, but she didn't have time to make a snappy retort as she hustled out of the house to her car. She had planned to look extra special tonight to make up for the minor tiff she and Sam had earlier. Now she was going to have to go for a quick spit and polish and hope that Sam was too consumed with the case to notice.

She parked in her driveway and blew into the house on a draft of cold air. Jake, Sandy and Josh were eating at the kitchen table, and she knew that Laura had already made plans to go out with friends.

"Hi," she said as she dumped her purse on the counter and bent over to kiss Josh's head. Then she darted down the hall, calling, "Bye!"

In her room, Maggie pulled on a pretty green sweater to highlight her eyes. She ran a brush through her auburn hair and yanked on a pair of skinny jeans that she paired with black high-heel leather boots. She checked her makeup, which was always minimal, and slicked on some lip gloss just as there was a knock on the front door. She glanced at her alarm clock. Seven o'clock on the dot. She might have known Sam would be right on time.

She dashed down the hallway only to see that Jake had answered the door and was shaking hands with Sam while Sandy stood with Josh, who was tugging on Sam's pant leg.

Sam hunkered low and was rewarded with a hug around the neck from the precocious toddler.

"Do you want to play trains with me?" Josh asked.

Sam's smile was warm and lit up his blue eyes in a way that made Maggie catch her breath.

"I'd like to, little buddy, but I promised I'd take your Aunt Maggie to dinner," he said. "Another time?"

"Promise," Josh said.

Sam stood and ruffled Josh's blond hair. "I promise."

"Have fun, kids," Jake said as he held the door open for them.

"Call if you're going to be late," Sandy said.

"She has a curfew," Jake said to Sam. "We would hate to have to ground her."

Maggie rolled her eyes at Sam, and he chuckled.

"Good night, *kids*," she said as she pulled on her coat and slipped out the door.

As they walked to the car, she looked at Sam. "Sorry about that. My family isn't used to me having dates."

He grinned. "Is it wrong that that makes me happy?"

He held open the door, and she slid into the passenger seat of his squad car.

"Are you on duty?" she asked.

"Always," he said.

He closed the door and circled around the car to the driver side. He got into the car and started the engine. Maggie felt a blast of heat shoot across her feet for which she was grateful.

As he reversed down the driveway, he braced his arm across the back of her seat. While he navigated the short drive, he glanced at her, and said, "So, do you want to tell me what you, Ginger and Claire were doing in Diane Jenkins's apartment tonight?"

Chapter 16

Maggie contemplated bluffing. But really, what was the point? Ginger had been right. St. Stanley was the size of a Q-tip, and Maggie should have known that Sam would hear about their visit to Diane's apartment.

"Are you mad?" she asked.

"Not as mad as I should be," he said. "What were you hoping to find?"

"Something that would tell us about her past," Maggie said.

"And you thought you'd be more skilled at searching someone's house than a trained professional?"

"No, but I hoped we'd get lucky," she said.

They were both quiet for a moment, and Maggie suspected she was about to have the worst date of her life. She had that *ick* feeling she always got when she felt guilty, and she really wasn't enjoying it.

"So, did you?" he asked. "Get lucky?"

"No," she said. "It was as if no one actually lived there."

"Indeed," he said.

Maggie studied his profile. She could see the muscle in his cheek moving; it was either clenching or having spasms. She wondered if she should call off their date. On top of the awkwardness and tension now between them, she also felt guilty about not being with Joanne. Claire was spending the night with her again, but Maggie felt like she should be taking a turn.

"Maybe we should postpone our date until things settle down," she said. She realized as soon as she said it that she didn't want to call it off, but she didn't want to spend an awkward, guilt-ridden evening either.

"Is that what you want?" Sam stopped at the stop sign that led away from her street and glanced at her.

"No! Um, I mean, no, but I . . . What do you want to do?"

"Honestly, I have been a cop long enough to know that the lines between working and not working are very blurry," he said. "If you get a chance to have dinner with a beautiful woman, then you take it, because you may not get another."

Maggie smiled at him. She couldn't help it. He'd called her beautiful and, coming from Sam . . . Well, his compliments always made her dizzy.

"Since you put it that way," she said. "Onward."

Sam grinned at her and turned left. They wound their way through town until they reached a small house on the edge of her neighborhood. Sam pulled into the driveway and switched the engine off.

Maggie glanced at the house and then at him. "Doesn't the Hall family live here?"

"They did," he said. "Until Mrs. Hall passed away and Mr. Hall went to live with his son in Richmond. We were on the force together."

"That's right," Maggie said. "I forgot Christopher Hall became a cop, too. How is he?"

"Married with two kids in college," he said. "He's retired and has his own security company now. When he heard I was coming back, he offered to rent me his dad's house since his dad was going to move in with him."

Maggie turned and looked at the small bungalow. It was white with black shutters and a red front door. The lawn was neatly mowed and the bushes trimmed, but it lacked a lived-in look and reminded her of Diane's apartment in that way. A wreath on the door or a swinging bench would help.

"I hope you don't mind," Sam said. "I thought I'd cook dinner and that way, if there is a break in the case and I have to go, we won't be running out of a restaurant in the middle of the meal."

"It's fine," Maggie assured him as he led her up the walkway to the house. "I didn't know you could cook."

"Mostly, it's bachelor food," he said. "Spaghetti with ketchup."

Maggie cringed, and he laughed.

"Don't worry," he said. "I turned it up a notch just for you."

"I'm honored," she said.

Sam studied her for a second; his eyes scanned her face as if trying to see inside her. Whatever he saw, he made no comment and Maggie didn't ask.

"Come on," he said. He held open the door and ushered her inside.

The first thing that struck Maggie was the lack of pictures on the walls. The furniture was very male, as in it was all brown leather, crowded around a huge television.

Sam led her through the living room and into a surprisingly modern kitchen with granite counters and copper pots hanging over an island in the middle of the room. A cozy dining nook with a round table and four chairs sat at the other end of the room overlooking a small but well-kept backyard.

The spotlight was on, and Maggie peered out the two French doors between the kitchen and the dining nook and noticed that there was a grill and an eating area on the small patio, and the lawn, although now brown from the winter, looked like it had been thick. There was no sign of a garden, just a plain wooden fence that enclosed the back.

A noise from near her feet sounded, and Maggie jumped back. One of the panels in the French door was actually a pet door. As it was pushed open, a bundle of gray-striped fur half fell and half tumbled onto the floor.

"Marshall Dillon," Sam said to the cat. "What have you been up to, buddy?"

The cat, which looked to be somewhere between a kitten and a cat, galloped toward Sam as he squatted down. The gray fur ball stood on his back legs and placed his front feet on Sam's knee. Sam leaned his head down and the two of them bumped foreheads, which Maggie took to be the cat's version of a high five or a fist bump.

It was impossibly charming, and she found she was grinning stupidly at Sam as he scooped the cat up and held him with one arm while he turned to look at Maggie.

"Marshall Dillon?" she asked.

"We like to watch old *Gunsmoke* episodes together," Sam explained. "And his stripes make an M on his forehead."

He held the cat out so Maggie could see the M, which did sit right over his eyes like an inquisitive unibrow.

"Marshall adopted me the day after I moved in," he said. "I tried keeping him in the house, but it didn't go well. He peed all over the place and shredded a pair of my pants."

He frowned at the cat, who blinked at him, the picture of innocence.

"So, he's nipped and tucked, tagged and microchipped, but I'm respecting his need to be a free spirit and letting him go outside."

"You sound like a worried parent," she said.

"I know." He looked chagrinned. "After all of these years on my own, having someone else to look after, well, it's scary."

Maggie lowered her head to hide her smile while she held out her hand for Marshall to inspect. He sniffed her and then rubbed the side of his face against her fingers. He started to purr, and Sam lifted his eyebrows in surprise.

"You're the first person he's taken to," he said. "He scratched Deputy Rourke when he stopped by the other day, but then again, Rourke doesn't smell as nice as you."

Sam leaned over the cat and kissed Maggie lightly on the lips. As always, it left Maggie breathless.

"I've wanted to do that since I picked you up," he said.

"Even though you're mad at me?" she asked.

Sam put the cat down and pulled Maggie into his arms.

"I'm always mad at you," he said. He kissed her again, more deeply this time. When he pulled back, he sighed. "And still I want to kiss you."

Maggie laughed. "So, we're okay?"

"I wouldn't go that far," he said. "We still need to talk."

"I thought that was my line," she said. "I'm the girl."

"Yeah, but I'm an evolved male, and I'm the one who's mad," he said.

"All righty, then," she said.

He pulled a chair out from the counter and directed her to sit. He took out a wine bottle and handed it to her for inspection. Marshall Dillon glanced between them and meowed piteously until Sam went to the pantry tucked into the corner of the kitchen and took out a can of cat food.

Maggie poured the wine while Sam fed the cat. It was such a moment of domesticity that she wondered if this was what the end of the day would always be like with Sam. Then she shook her head. This was their first official date since they were kids. She really needed not to get ahead of herself.

Once Marshall Dillon was happily noshing his dinner, Sam washed his hands and set about making theirs. Maggie sipped her wine while she watched him. It was odd to have a man making dinner for her, and she realized none ever had before.

When she and Charlie were married, she had done all of the cooking because his job with the sheriff's department had kept his hours in constant rotation. She didn't date for years after he passed, because she was still grieving and her time was spent mostly providing for Laura. When she did finally start dating, it was always to go out to dinner or movies or an event. Sadly, she had never dated anyone long enough to have them cook for her. She had just never met anyone who'd made it past the third date.

Maggie watched as Sam put fettuccini into a big pot of

boiling water. While that cooked, he prepped a salad. Maggie watched his hands move through the motions of slicing and dicing and tossing the salad.

When he was finished he put it on the small table for four, which she noted was set for two, and he lit a candle. Okay, the man was getting points for ambiance. He moved the wine bottle to the table and then returned to the stove where he melted a stick of butter in a skillet and added an equal amount of cream. He took a big bowl of freshly grated parmesan out of the fridge and then added just a bit of ground pepper to the butter-and-cream sauce. It looked wonderful, and Maggie surreptitiously checked her chin to make sure she wasn't drooling.

Sam picked up a fork and used it to twirl a piece of fettuccini out of the pot. He flicked the pasta at the wall and it stuck.

He grinned at Maggie. "It's ready!"

Maggie gave him a confused look.

"When I first moved to Richmond, I took a job in an Italian restaurant. That was how the chef tested the pasta," he said.

He drained the rest of the pasta into a big metal colander and then poured the cream sauce into a huge pasta bowl followed by half of the parmesan.

He glanced into the bowl and then back at Maggie. "They're getting to know each other."

Maggie glanced into the bowl, too. It looked and smelled divine.

"Anyway, we used to make fettuccini Alfredo right at the table," he said. "I thought it might give me that wow factor with you to show off the old skills."

"Oh, you've got it," Maggie assured him as he poured the pasta into the bowl and then tossed on the rest of the parmesan and used a big pair of tongs to lightly mix it all up.

"Dinner is served," he said, and he led the way to the small table.

Maggie took the seat across from him and dished her own salad while he dug into the fettuccini, then they switched. Usually on dates she felt overly self-conscious about any lags in conversation, but with Sam the quiet felt natural. Of course, it also felt like he was gearing up for a lecture.

She was surprised to find that she didn't mind. If she was honest, she figured she deserved one. She really wished she could say that they had found something in Diane's apartment, something that would give them a clue to her past. Since they hadn't, she figured she might as well go for broke and ask him about what had been bothering her ever since she'd been in Diane's apartment.

"So I was wondering," she began, pausing to take a sip of wine to fortify herself, "about those photographs you found."

Sam looked at her and one of his eyebrows slowly rose higher than the other.

"You're kidding, right?"

"'Fraid not," she said. "When I was in the apartment, I was thinking about the pictures, and I remembered that you said some of them were of her in her apartment. Right?"

"You don't really think I'm going to talk about this, do you?" he asked.

"Yes, I do," she said.

Sam tucked into his pasta and Maggie did the same. She didn't know if he was just avoiding the conversation or if he was stalling to build up his argument. She followed his example and forked up some of her pasta.

She popped it into her mouth and then her eyes went wide. It was a good thing she had a mouthful of food, or she might have proposed to him on the spot. The fettuccini was amazing, and she kept on eating, forgetting that she had just asked him a question.

When she'd taken several more bites, she glanced up to find Sam watching her with a small smile.

She gestured at her plate with her fork. "This is fantastic. I'm in awe of your culinary skills, truly."

"Thank you," he said. "I'm still not telling you about the photos."

"What?" she protested. "You have to."

"No, I don't."

"Okay, *have to* is too strong a phrase," she said.

"Agreed," he said.

She noticed the muscle in his jaw was clenching again. He put down his fork and met her gaze with his. His blue eyes were intense, and the mouthful of pasta she had just swallowed went down hard.

"Maggie, this case is dangerous," he said. "Whoever killed Diane is a psychopath who likely viewed her as an object and enjoyed having her be helpless against him."

Maggie shuddered at the mental picture, but Sam continued, as if determined to make her afraid.

"Strangulation isn't the easiest way to kill someone," he said. "A killer uses strangulation because he or she enjoys complete control over his victim."

Maggie took a sip of wine. "So you don't think it was Joanne, do you?"

"No, I checked through her alibi again, and it's pretty tight," he said.

"And Michael?" Maggie asked. "You don't really think it was him, either?"

Sam sighed. "I don't know. Until he wakes up and tells us what he knows, I can't say."

"But it couldn't be him," Maggie protested. "He was unconscious in a pool of blood."

"Maybe," Sam said. "It could be that Diane whacked him in the head while he was strangling her but he didn't pass out until after she was dead."

Maggie shook her head. She refused to believe it.

"See? This is why you need to show me the pictures," Maggie said. "You've been away for years, but I haven't. I know these people, I know this town. I might see something in the photos that you've missed. I can help you."

"Maggie, I don't want you anywhere near this case," Sam said. "I don't want you in danger."

"I appreciate that," she said.

She reached across the table and covered his hand with hers. She meant it. She did appreciate that he wanted to keep her safe. It meant a lot to her to have someone who felt that way about her again, but there was more at stake here than just her safety.

Sam turned his hand under hers and wrapped her fingers with his.

"I just got you back," he said. "I won't risk losing you again."

The affection in his gaze mingled with his fierce protectiveness made her heart melt, and it was all she could do to stay in her seat and not fling herself into his arms. She had to make one important point first.

"If you want to keep me safe, then keep me informed," she said. "If there is a killer among us, I'm more likely than you to know them. Trust me, Sam, and let me help."

He squeezed her fingers in his while he studied her face.

"You're just going to keep digging and digging no matter what I say, aren't you?"

"Yup."

He sighed. "I really hate this."

"I know."

"I can't tell you everything," he said. "I can't put the case in jeopardy, but I'll tell you about the pictures."

"Thank you."

He groaned and then gave her a small smile as he released her hand and they resumed eating dinner.

"Yes, some of the photos were of her in her apartment," he confirmed.

"Were they taken from the field behind the house, the old house next door or the plumbing-supply shop across the street?" Maggie asked.

Again Sam looked at her with one eyebrow raised.

"What? I looked out the windows while we were at her apartment," she said. "I was trying to see where the killer might have watched her from."

"See? This is what I'm talking about," he said. "What if the killer was watching you? What if he saw you poking around in there? You may have made yourself a target."

A shiver scurried up Maggie's back like a spider climbing up its web.

"You're trying to scare me," she said.

"Is it working?"

"A little."

"Good," he said. He dabbed his mouth with his napkin and drank some wine. "From the angle, I think the picture had to be from the roof of the plumbing-supply store."

Maggie opened her mouth to speak, but he held his hand up to stop her.

"I already spoke to Henry Colbert, the owner, and he said the upper stories are just for storage, and no one has been on his roof since he had his air conditioner serviced last summer."

Maggie chewed a bite of tomato from her salad while she thought about what he'd said. Just because Henry didn't know someone had been on the roof didn't mean they hadn't been there.

She was about to say as much when she heard her phone ringing inside her purse.

"Excuse me," she said, and Sam nodded. Normally she wouldn't check her phone during a meal, but she wanted to be sure Joanne was all right.

She opened her purse and dug out her phone. It was a text message from Ginger. It was short and to the point.

She glanced from the phone to Sam to find him watching her.

She blew out a breath, and said, "Michael is awake."

Chapter 17

"I'll drive," Sam said.

They hurriedly put away the remnants of their dinner and hustled out to the car. Sam didn't use the siren but he drove at a brisk clip across town to the hospital.

He parked close to the building, and together they rode the elevator up to five and then jogged down the hall toward the ICU. Claire was waiting, but there was no sign of Joanne or Ginger.

"Maggie, I'm so glad you're here," Claire said as she hugged her. "Hi, Sam."

"What happened?" Maggie asked. "Is Michael okay?"

By this she meant was he mentally impaired from the blow he'd taken to his head, but she felt this was the more tactful way to ask.

"I don't know," Claire said. "Ginger went in with Joanne about a half hour ago, but they haven't come out yet. All I know is that the doctor came and told Joanne that he was awake and asked her to go and see him."

"I'm going to call back there," Sam said. He went to the phone on the wall that allowed visitors in the waiting room to call the nurse's station in the ICU. He dialed quickly, and Maggie heard him identify himself and ask to see Michael Claramotta.

After a moment, he hung up and looked at Maggie. "I'm going in."

"Can we come with you?" she asked.

He shook his head regretfully. "Only two are allowed at a time. Ginger is on her way out."

Maggie nodded. She knew it would do no good to argue. This was the hospital's rule, not Sam's.

The doors opened and Ginger came out. She saw Sam and hesitated. It looked to Maggie like she wanted to say something and then thought better of it. Instead, she nodded at him and squeezed his forearm as she passed him. Sam returned her nod and hurried through the open doors.

"How is he?" Maggie asked. Her chest felt tight, and she realized she was holding her breath.

"He's loopy," Ginger said. "The meds they've had him on haven't worn off, and he thinks he's at a party. He doesn't know why he's here and, as far as we can tell, he doesn't remember anything."

"Not even Joanne or the baby?" Claire asked, horrified.

"No, sorry," Ginger said. "He remembers who he is and all of that, but he doesn't remember what happened to him."

"Did Joanne tell him?" Maggie asked.

"She's waiting for the doctor to give the okay," Ginger said. "The doctor wants to wait until he's a little more lucid before hitting him with bad news and potentially causing his condition to worsen."

"So, he doesn't know that he was attacked and that Diane was murdered," Claire said. "Wow, I think the doctor is spot-on. Who knows how that kind of shock would affect his recovery, besides which I'm not really sure how you work all of that into a conversation."

"Do you think Sam will question him?" Ginger asked Maggie.

"I'm sure that's why he went back there." Maggie stared hard at the door as if she could see beyond it and find out what was happening.

"Don't worry," Ginger said. "Sam's a pro. He'll handle it well."

Maggie paced. She didn't know what else to do with her nervous energy. If Michael didn't remember anything, then they were no better off than they were when he was unconscious. Of course, he was better off, and she was grateful for that for Joanne's sake.

While she paced she thought about the photos, the lack of a personal history for Diane and the possible motives of her two friends. She refused to entertain the thought that either Michael or Joanne could be Diane's killer. It was ridiculous, but if it wasn't them, then who was it? Who'd had a grudge against Diane?

As she crossed the room, she had to stop to make way for Ginger, who was pacing across her path, and then again for Claire, who was pacing around the room in a circle. She felt as if she were dancing at the ball again, except they were all missing their partners.

Maggie stumbled to a halt. The ball. The gowns. Britney

Bergstrom. The idea flashed through her mind with the speed of a strobe light.

How could she have forgotten Britney Bergstrom threatening Diane in the shop the day before the ball? And then at the ball, Maggie had seen Britney with her group of friends mocking Diane and trying to make her miserable until Ginger's boys and Laura had formed a protective circle around Diane, making it clear that she was not to be bullied.

"Maggie, you're in the way," Ginger said as she went to walk around her.

"Sorry, I just had a crazy thought," Maggie said.

"Do tell," Ginger said as she and Claire came to stand beside her.

Maggie opened her mouth to speak, but the automatic door opened and Sam stepped back into the room, causing Maggie to forget what she'd been about to say.

He looked unsatisfied, and Maggie knew that Michael hadn't been able to tell him anything of use.

"How did it go?" she asked.

"Not good," Sam said. "He kept asking me if his bow tie was tied just right. He thinks he's back at the Madison ball. Dr. Graber seems optimistic that his memory will come back, but he wants me to wait to question him."

"I want to go see him," Maggie said.

"I thought you might." Sam gave her an understanding smile. "I told Joanne I'd send you in. He's in room three thirty-six."

"Thanks," she said. She kissed his cheek and hurried into the ICU.

The ICU was a circle of glass rooms built around the nurses' station, which sat in the middle. Maggie checked the numbers on the doors she passed. She saw several patients who appeared to be asleep. They were alone with no one standing vigil by their beds. It made her sad, and she wondered how many patients came in here alone and left alone.

Michael's room was toward the back. She saw Joanne standing by his bed. They were holding hands and looking at each other as if each were trying to memorize the other's face on the off chance one of them should blink out again.

Maggie hated to interrupt, but she knew visiting hours were ending in minutes, and they were about to be chucked out of the hospital for the night.

"Knock, knock," she said.

Michael rolled his head on his pillow, and Joanne glanced up. They both smiled. Michael's smile was weak, but Joanne beamed at her.

"He woke up!" she cried. Maggie had known her friend was worried, but she hadn't appreciated just how much until she saw how relieved Joanne was.

Maggie crossed the room and hugged Joanne and then Michael.

"It's good to see you," she said. She patted his hand, and he sighed.

"You, too, Maggie," he said. "Although aren't you a bit underdressed?"

Maggie glanced at Joanne, who was fretting her lip.

"We're at the ball," she said, and she tapped her finger to her temple. Maggie gave her a nod of understanding.

"You're right," Maggie said to Michael. "I'll go change in a minute."

"Good plan," Michael said. "You don't want to miss the

mini quiches that they're passing around. They're loaded with bacon and cheddar."

Maggie gave a faint chuckle that she hoped didn't sound as forced as it felt. Michael peered out the door of his room as if expecting a waiter with a tray of quiches to appear at any moment.

"Did the doctor say when he can leave?" she asked Joanne.

"No, they're worried about the memory loss," she said. "He doesn't even realize he's in the hospital."

"Who's in the hospital?" Michael asked.

"You," Joanne said.

Michael gave her a funny look, and then his face cleared, and he said, "You're teasing me."

Joanne sighed and patted his hand. "Just so."

Michael's face looked pale and tired under the bandage wrapped around his head, and he closed his eyes and seemed to drift to sleep. Maggie gave Joanne a worried look, but Joanne shook her head.

"It's okay," she whispered. "He's been doing that on and off since he woke up."

"I'm sorry, ladies, but visiting hours are over," a nurse said as she entered the room.

"So soon?" Joanne asked.

The nurse gave her a sympathetic look. "I promise to keep a very close watch on him."

"Thank you," Joanne said.

"I'll give you some alone time," Maggie said. She slipped out of the room with a wave and made her way back to the waiting room.

The others were still there. She noted that they were sitting and not pacing anymore. She took an empty seat next to Sam.

"So, Michael's still at the ball," she said.

"Yup, and he didn't approve of my attire," Sam said.

"Mine either," Maggie said. "He was very concerned that I'd miss out on the mini quiches."

They shared an awkward chuckle.

"At least he's awake," Sam said.

"How long will you give him?" Maggie asked. "You know, before you have to tell him."

"I don't know," Sam said. He sounded reluctant, and Maggie suspected he would much rather be operating with absolutes, such as knowing that Michael would remember everything tomorrow.

The doors to the waiting room opened and Joanne stepped through. She looked happy with a side of fretful, and Maggie knew it was worrying her to leave Michael when he had just woken up.

"He'll be all right," Ginger said. She hugged Joanne, and said, "I'm babysitting you tonight, and I promise we'll call the hospital every half hour to check on him if you want."

Joanne's eyes got watery, and she hugged Ginger close. "Thanks. I'd say I'll be all right on my own, but it would be a big fat lie."

"I can stay with you, too," Claire said as she joined the embrace, which for Claire was big, as she wasn't a hugger as a rule.

"Me, too," Maggie offered, jumping into the group hug.

"Aw, thanks," Joanne sniffled. "You gals are the best, but

I think it might be good if we work you all in on a rotating basis. I don't know how long this will go on, and I don't want you to get sick of babysitting me."

The four of them stood in a huddle with their arms around one another.

"Sounds like a plan," Claire said.

"We're going to get through this," Ginger said.

"Remember," Maggie said, "it's one for all and all for one, unless it's a two-for-one sale on Italian shoes, and then it's every girl for herself."

Joanne laughed as Maggie had hoped she would, and the huddle broke up. Sam stood watching them with a look of bemusement, and Maggie moved to stand beside him.

"Ready to go?" she asked.

"Yes," he said. He led her toward the door, and Maggie felt the others fall in behind them. Then he leaned close, and whispered so only she could hear him, "It really is going to be okay."

Maggie squeezed his arm to let him know she'd heard him and appreciated it.

Once they reached the parking lot, they waved to the others, and Sam opened the passenger door for her. Maggie's phone rang as she was getting into the car. She fished it out of her purse and saw Max's number.

While Sam circled the car to get in, she answered, "Hello?"

"Maggie, it's Max."

"Hi, Max. What's up?"

"I'm not sure, but I think I might have a lead on where Diane Jenkins is from," he said.

Chapter 18

"Really?" Maggie asked. "How?"

"Bianca and I were talking about what happened at the deli, and she said something about Diane being from New England," Max said. "I asked her how she knew that, and she said when they had a conversation at the ball, Diane said something about missing coffee milk."

Maggie glanced at Sam as he got into the car beside her and started up the engine. When he glanced at her, she mouthed the name *Max*, and he nodded.

"You've lost me," she said into the phone. "First of all, what is coffee milk?"

"I know, right?" Max asked. "I'd never heard of it either, but as a kid Bianca spent a summer in Newport, Rhode Island, studying classical piano at a music conservatory, and she remembered that the locals all drink the stuff. It's like chocolate milk but they make it with a coffee-flavored syrup instead."

"Weird," Maggie said.

"Yeah," Max agreed. "Anyway, Bianca said that when she met Diane at the ball, she caught a trace of her accent and asked her if she'd ever had coffee milk. She said Diane looked wistful and said it was one of the things she missed most from home."

"So, Diane is from New England?" Maggie asked. She saw Sam's head whip around to stare at her, and she held up her hand to indicate that she was still listening and to hold his questions.

"More specifically, she's from Rhode Island, or at least she lived there at one time," Max said. "Coffee milk is apparently a Rhode Island thing."

"Huh. That's amazing," Maggie said. "Nice work, Max."

"I was going to call Sam, but I don't have his direct number, and a little bird named Laura told me you were having dinner with him. How's that going, by the way?"

Maggie felt her face get warm. She was so not used to being in a relationship and having people ask her about it.

"Very well, thank you," she said. "In fact, he's right here, so I'll just go and tell him what you told me. Probably, he's going to want to talk to Bianca and see if she remembers anything else."

"We figured. Tell him to call my cell whenever," Max said. "Bye, Maggie."

"Bye, Max, and thanks."

Sam stopped the car in front of her house and turned to face her. "I get the feeling you're about to make my day."

"Could be," she said with a smile. Then she told him what

Max had told her. Sam didn't interrupt but listened intently, frowning a bit as he did.

When Maggie was finished, he looked at her and asked, "Have you ever heard of coffee milk?"

"No."

Sam got out of the car and circled around the hood to Maggie's side. He opened the door for her and Maggie climbed out. Sam put his arm around her as he walked her to the door.

"Want to come in for dessert?" she asked.

Sam looked at her with his eyebrows raised, and she laughed. "I meant pecan pie."

He leaned forward and kissed her.

"Tempting," he said when he stepped back. "Very tempting. But I think I'm going to head back to the station and see what I can find out about any women missing from Rhode Island who fit Diane Jenkins's description."

"I figured," Maggie said. "Do you think it's too flimsy of a lead?"

Sam shrugged. "Sometimes an entire case will turn on the tiniest bit of information."

"Good luck," Maggie said. "I hope you find something."

"Me, too. Call you tomorrow?"

Maggie nodded. Sam stood watching her until she closed the door behind her. She waved from the window as he got back into his car and reversed out of her driveway. With a return wave he was gone. For a second, she stood frozen in time. She remembered being exactly here in this spot waving to her late husband, Charlie, as he left.

She closed her eyes and sighed. It had been almost twenty years, but still the shock of losing Charlie hit her low and deep. Was she crazy to be dating the sheriff? To take a chance on losing a man that she lo—*cared for* . . . Maggie thought she must be out of her mind.

A hand landed on her shoulder, and she jumped and let out a yelp as she whipped around to find Laura standing behind her.

"Sorry," Laura said. "I didn't mean to startle you."

"It's okay," Maggie said. "I was just thinking."

"That dating a police officer is risky, and you don't want to go through what you went through when dad was killed?"

Maggie frowned. "Was I thinking out loud?"

"No, I just figured that had to occur to you at some point, and given that Sam just drove off, probably to work on solving Diane's murder, well, it seemed likely that you'd be thinking that."

"How exactly did you get so smart?"

"Quality genetic material."

Maggie laughed and hugged her daughter close.

"I love you."

"I love you, too."

"How have things been at the shop?" Maggie asked.

"Busy," Laura said. "Which is great, because it keeps my mind off . . . you know."

"How about we have a girls' night with popcorn and a *Gilmore Girls* marathon?" Maggie asked.

"Oh, I'd love to, but I have a date," Laura said.

It was then that Maggie noticed her daughter was wearing her favorite black leather boots over skinny jeans and a deep purple jersey knit top.

"Are those my skinny jeans?" Maggie asked.

"Maybe," Laura said with a sheepish shrug. "Hey, if you

don't want me to borrow your clothes don't have such fabulous taste in just my size."

Maggie chuckled and then frowned. "It's kind of late to be just going out, isn't it?"

"It's only nine thirty," Laura said. "We're going to see a band over at the Daily Grind."

"A band is playing at Pete's coffee shop?" Maggie tried to picture this.

"Yeah, they asked to have a CD launch party there, and Pete said yes. He's pretty cool."

"So, who are you going with?" Maggie asked. She hated to give the third degree, but this was her baby girl. No one was good enough as far as she was concerned.

"A customer from the shop actually," Laura said. "Blake Caulfield."

"The guy who bought the Anne Barge gown for his fiancée?" Maggie asked.

"He returned it, remember? It seems they broke up," Laura said.

Maggie frowned. She didn't want Laura to be Blake's rebound girl no matter how nice he had seemed.

"Mom, don't worry. I know better than to date a guy who is pining for someone else. We're just going as friends, and we're meeting Max, Bianca and Aaron there, so it's more of a group thing."

"Well, that sounds like it will be fun," she said. "What kind of music is it?"

"I'm not sure," Laura said. "Bianca likes them, so it has to be something good, right?"

"Hmm, given her love of classical music, that could go either way," Maggie said.

There was a knock on the door, and they both turned toward it.

"That's him," Laura said. She scooped up her jacket and purse en route to the door.

She opened the door with one hand while she shrugged into her coat with the other.

"Hi, Blake, come on in," she said.

Blake entered the room, and Maggie smiled in welcome. He really was quite a handsome young man, and she remembered how he had made Claire laugh when she was trying on her gown by pretending to have a heart attack at the sight of her.

"It's good to see you again, Blake," she said.

"You, too, Mrs. Gerber," he said. "Your daughter and her friends have been kind enough to include me in their plans. I really appreciate it."

"It's our pleasure," Laura assured him. "Blake is studying to be an attorney at Max's alma mater. They've been comparing war stories."

"Really? Good for you. I was sorry to hear about . . ."

Maggie's voice trailed off. It belatedly occurred to her that his terminated engagement might not be a topic he wished to discuss.

"The change in my Facebook status?" Blake asked with a wry smile.

"Sorry," Maggie said. "That was tactless of me."

"It's all right," he assured her. "As my mom said, it's better that I found out now that she was interested in someone else than after we were married."

"Most definitely," Laura agreed. "Hey, we'd better go or Max and Bianca will think we stood them up."

"Have fun," Maggie said.

"I'll have her home by midnight," Blake said.

Maggie smiled at him. Sense of humor, check; polite, check; handsome, check; law student, check; now, if only he didn't have that pesky broken heart, he'd be perfect.

Laura rolled her eyes at the two of them. She kissed her mother's cheek, and said, "Don't wait up."

Maggie waved them out and closed the door behind them. The house was very quiet, and she suspected that Sandy and Jake had gone to bed right after Josh. The young couple was spending a lot of time holed up in their room, catching up on the months they'd missed.

Now Laura had met a nice young man, and she and Sam were on track. If it weren't for the horrific murder of Diane Jenkins and the injury to Michael Claramotta, she could almost think this was going to be a happy Christmas. Almost.

Chapter 19

Maggie woke up early the next morning. She had heard Laura come in just before midnight, and she was grateful to have such a considerate daughter who didn't stay out overly late, knowing that Maggie would worry.

She peeked her head into Laura's room to see that she was still asleep. Her lips were slightly parted and her breathing was even and regular; yes, even after all of these years, Maggie still checked to see if her baby was breathing. Laura's red-brown hair spread across her pillow, and she had one arm draped over her eyes as if to ward off the impending daylight.

Maggie closed the door quietly behind her and went to the kitchen to find a fresh pot of coffee already brewed. She glanced around the kitchen and found it empty, but then she saw Jake sitting out on the sunporch with the newspaper.

She poured herself a cup and went to join him. He had

the sports page draped over his lap, but his gaze was directed out the window, and she wondered what he was seeing.

"Mornin', Jake," she said as she sat in the chair beside his. "How are you?"

He rubbed his eyes, and Maggie saw the faint trace of damp on his cheeks.

"I'm sorry," she said. "I didn't mean to intrude."

She half rose out of her seat, but he held up his hand, gesturing for her to stop.

"It's okay," he said. He took a bracing sip of coffee and then gave her a wry smile. "I was just watching the sunrise and giving thanks that I'm here."

"Aw, Jake." Maggie put her cup down on the table and hugged him. "We're grateful that you're here, too."

"Thanks," he said, and hugged her back.

She cupped his face in her hands and kissed his forehead as if he were no bigger than Josh before she sat back down.

"Now tell me about the house," she said.

Jake's face lit up with excitement as he told her all about it and their hopes to add to their little family and build a swing set for Josh and his future brothers or sisters. It made Maggie's heart sing to hear of their plans. Sandy and Jake were due for a whole lot of good in their lives, and she was delighted to see it come to fruition.

When Sandy joined them a bit later, she was carrying Maggie's phone.

"Your phone was ringing," she said. "But I missed it."

"Oh, thanks," Maggie said. She glanced at it, wondering who would have called her so early. The number was Sam's, and after her heart did a little happy cartwheel, she realized he would only be calling her at this hour to tell her something bad.

She excused herself and went into the front room to return his call.

His deep voice answered on the third ring, "Mornin', Maggie."

"Hi, Sam. Please tell me you called to tell me about a killer sale on bath towels."

"You got the killer part right," he said. His voice was low "It's not good news, Maggie."

Maggie felt her heart thump hard with dread.

"What did you find out?"

The sigh on the other end of the line was heavy, and Maggie suspected that Sam had been up all night.

"There is a woman from Rhode Island who fits Diane's description who was reported missing by her aunt a few months ago."

"Do you think it's her?"

"I don't know for sure, but in talking to the detective who took the missing-person's report, I'd say it's likely."

They were both silent. Maggie sensed there was something that Sam wasn't telling her. This case had already caused friction between them. She knew it had the potential to fracture their tentative relationship. Their best line of defense was going to have to be communication.

"What aren't you telling me, Sam?" she asked. "If we're going to get through this, I need you to tell me what you can."

"I suppose it's better coming from me than the media," he said.

"The media?" she asked.

"It's going to get bad, Maggie," he said. "If our Diane Jenkins is the same woman who is missing from Rhode Island, then her real name in Leann Winthrop and she recently took a restraining order out on a man."

"Oh no. Do you think he found her here?" Maggie asked.

"That's where it gets complicated," Sam said. "The restraining order is against Michael Claramotta."

Chapter 20

"What?" she asked. "But that's impossible!"

"Let's just hope there's another Michael Claramotta living in the Ocean State," Sam said.

"Do you really think that name is that common?" Maggie asked. She could hear the panic in her voice and she knew that Sam could hear it, too.

"It'll be okay, Maggie," he said. "We'll figure it out."

"But how could she have a restraining order against him if she was working for him? And if this Leann person isn't Diane, then why did *she* have one against Michael?"

Maggie was loading up for more scattershot questions when Sam cut her off.

"Breathe, Maggie, breathe," he said. "We'll get it sorted. I promise."

"Are you going to see Michael?"

"In about an hour."

"Can I meet you there?" she asked. "Joanne might need the support."

"That'd be good," he said. "Maggie, for what it's worth, I'm sorry."

"Me, too," she said. "But I have to believe that this is just some kind of crazy coincidence. It's unthinkable otherwise."

Sam was silent, and she knew his years in law enforcement had given him glimpses into situations that were even crazier than this one, although she had a hard time imagining it.

"See you in an hour," he said.

"All right," she said.

She ended the call and hurried to her room to get dressed. She had to believe that this was all just some sort of insane misunderstanding, but deep down Maggie had never believed in coincidences.

When she saw Sam arrive at the hospital just minutes after she did, it took all of her self-control not to pepper him with more questions.

She and Joanne were seated in the waiting room, as the nurse had just sent Joanne out of Michael's room while they did some more tests. According to Joanne, Michael hadn't woken up yet, so she had no idea if he had miraculously regained his memory during the night or not.

Maggie knew that, with the new information he had, Sam wasn't going to be able to keep the truth from Michael any longer.

"Hi, Sam," she said.

"Hi, Maggie." His eyes rested on her briefly, and then he turned to Joanne. "How are you, Joanne?"

She didn't bother to answer but instead gave him a fret-ful look, and asked, "We're going to have to tell him today, aren't we?"

"I'm afraid so," he said. "New information is coming in, and I can't hold off any longer. I'll check with his doctor first, of course, but yes, I am going to have to question him about the attack."

Joanne closed her eyes for a moment as if bracing herself for what was to come.

"All right," she said. "Can I be there? In case he needs me?"

Sam considered her for a moment. "All right."

Maggie shot him a worried look. Would he tell her about the restraining order? She supposed he had to, but she was worried for her friend. She didn't see that going well no matter how he explained it.

The doors to the ICU opened and Dr. Graber entered the room. Sam went to talk to him and, after a moment, the doctor waved Joanne over to join them. Not knowing if she was allowed in on the conversation, Maggie waited a few feet away, wondering what the doctor's verdict would be.

After what seemed like a long time, the doctor nodded, and he and Sam shook hands. The doctor disappeared back into the ICU, and Sam leaned down and spoke softly to Joanne. Maggie wondered if he was telling her about the restraining order. Given that Joanne was nodding and look-ing very calm, Maggie assumed that he wasn't.

"Mrs. Claramotta," the nurse called from the open door. "You can come back in now."

Not wanting to be left out, Maggie moved to join them, and the three of them walked toward the door. The nurse frowned, but Sam said, "It's official police business. I need these two ladies with me."

She gave him a quick nod, and Maggie thought it must be nice to get your way just by saying *official police business*.

When they entered the room, Michael was propped up in bed, looking better than he had the night before but still drained and a bit pasty. Joanne hurried across the room and took his hand.

He must have sensed something, because he glanced at her and then at Sam. "Why am I here? What happened?"

"Everything is fine," Joanne said. Things were so obviously not fine that even a complete stranger could have guessed she was lying. "Sam just needs to talk to you."

"Oh, all right," Michael said. He seemed to relax a bit. "What can I do for you?"

"Have any memories of how you hit your head come back yet?" Sam asked.

"No, the last thing I remember is being at the Madison ball," Michael said, and gave a slow shake of his head.

Sam heaved a sigh. "Michael, I have some bad news."

Michael leaned up and immediately looked at Joanne and then at her rounded belly. Seeing his fear, she patted his hand, and said, "No, it's not me. The baby and I are fine."

He sank back down into his pillows with relief. Maggie guessed that, in his mind, so long as Joanne and the baby were okay, nothing else mattered.

"Your employee Diane Jenkins is dead," Sam said.

"What? How?" Michael asked. His forehead wrinkled with concern, and he glanced at Joanne as if needing her to confirm what Sam had said.

"It's true." Joanne gave him a sad nod, and he put his hand over his eyes as if he couldn't believe what he was hearing.

"How?" he repeated.

Sam was watching him closely as if cataloging his every move. Maggie wondered if he was trying to see if Michael was lying. She could have told him not to bother. She knew Michael, and the shock and bewilderment on his face were genuine.

"She was strangled," Sam said.

The air came out of Michael in a shocked whoosh, and Joanne stood and put her arm around him.

"No!" he said and shook his head. "No, it can't be."

"I'm sorry, Michael, it's true," Joanne said. "We found you—" Her voice cracked, as if the weight of the bad news were too much for it. She cleared her throat and continued. "Maggie and I came into the back of the shop, and you were lying on the floor in a pool of blood and Diane was just a few feet away from you, strangled with her apron strings."

"Is that . . . ?" Michael's voice was a whisper, and he reached up to feel the bandages on his head.

"Yes, we think that's how you cracked your head," Joanne said. "I didn't want to tell you all of this until you were stronger."

"Oh god, Diane," Michael's voice was a croak, and his eyes looked watery. Sam watched him, and Maggie felt her heart lurch at the guilt on Michael's face. "I tried to warn her, but she wouldn't listen."

"Listen to what?" Joanne asked. "What are you saying, Michael?"

Maggie glanced at Joanne's face and saw the devastation

and betrayal creep across her features even while she clung to her husband's hand, obviously hoping that this was all just some sort of mistake.

Michael turned to look at Sam. "It was him, wasn't it?"

"Him who?" Sam asked evenly.

"The man who was stalking her," Michael said. "I told her that she couldn't just hide, that she had to go to the police, especially when those pictures showed up. We had a terrible fight about it. Oh god, poor Diane."

"Who was stalking her, Michael?" Sam asked. His voice was tight and Maggie knew that Michael's answer was critical.

"I don't know," Michael said.

"Really?" Sam asked. His face was hard. "Because she took a restraining order out on you."

Chapter 21

"What?" Michael lurched forward and then winced. He fell back against his pillows. "That's ridiculous. I was helping her."

"Michael, what is going on?" Joanne asked. Her voice was high and frightened, and she let go of his hand and wrapped her arms protectively about her middle.

"Oh, hon, I wanted to tell you, but I didn't want you to worry," he said. "Diane is a friend of Brody Schuster. Remember, he and I used to work at Decusati's Deli back in the neighborhood."

"Brody? Didn't he move to Rhode Island to open a deli there?" she asked.

"Yes, and Diane—her real name is Leann something— is . . . was one of his employees. Well, some crazy guy started to stalk her. He would take pictures of her and then send them to her, so Brody asked me if she could come down here and work for me for a while. We made up a new name for her and I paid her in cash, so there was no paper trail."

Michael paused and gave Sam a defiant look. "I know that's not legal, but I don't care. We were trying to keep her safe."

"I'm not the IRS," Sam said. "You can take that up with your accountant. Who was the guy? What was his name?"

"Diane, er, Leann didn't know," Michael said. "But it was getting dangerous for her. Brody told me that one night someone followed her home from work. He ran her off the road, but a tow truck happened by, and the person sped off. The driver of the tow truck got the license plate, but it turned out the car had just been reported stolen. That's when Brody called me to see if I could hide Diane for a while."

The room was silent for a moment, and Maggie glanced at Joanne to see how she was taking this. Her lips were clamped tight, and she was shaking.

"Are you all right, Joanne?" Michael asked.

"You should have told me," she said.

Michael gave her an imploring glance. "I'm sorry. I would have. I've never kept a secret from you, but I didn't want to alarm you and risk the baby."

Joanne nodded, but Maggie could see that she was struggling when she didn't take Michael's hand again. In fact, she put about a foot of space between them. Michael looked crestfallen, and Maggie could tell that he felt Joanne's ire too.

"Why didn't she file a report with me?" Sam asked. "We could have given her added protection."

"We argued about it. The day of the Madison ball, we

found a bunch of pictures shoved into the delivery van, and we knew he'd found her."

Michael stared out the window remembering. He looked back and sighed.

"She freaked out, and I told her she had to tell the police, but she was afraid," he said. "She didn't know who he was or why he was fixated on her, and her biggest fear was that he was a person of power and the police would believe him over her."

"That makes no sense," Maggie said, "since whoever was stalking her obviously followed her from Rhode Island. Why would she think he had any power here?"

"Probably, because he found her," he said.

"I'm going to need to talk to your friend, Brody," Sam said.

Michael nodded, and then he frowned. "I don't understand the restraining order. How could there be one against me in a place I've never been?"

"We'll have to check into it," Sam said. "I don't like it, but maybe it will give us the lead we need to catch this guy."

"Are you sure it's a guy?" Maggie asked. "Did Diane— or rather, Leann—know for a fact that it was a guy?"

Michael shook his head. "No, the local police checked out all of her old boyfriends, but they were all cleared. She doesn't do social networks, so it wasn't anyone online. The only contact she had with the person were the pictures of her that he sent. And he photographed her everywhere: at her job, at the gym, in her apartment. It was creepy."

"Michael, do you have any memory of what happened in the deli?" Sam asked. His voice was low, and Maggie could tell he was trying to sound casual, but there was nothing casual in the intensity of his stare.

Michael studied the ceiling, and Maggie could feel him trying to piece it together, trying to grab at any scrap of memory that could be lodged in his head. He punched the mattress by his hip in frustration.

"I've got nothing," he said. "The last thing I remember was hearing a noise in the kitchen and leaving my office to go and check it out. Oh god, I feel like I failed her. She was supposed to be safe here in St. Stanley."

His anguish made Maggie's heart hurt, and Joanne must have felt it, too, because she took his hand again and squeezed it tight.

"You did your best," she said.

"Did I?" Michael asked. He glanced at each of them in turn, and Maggie knew the guilt was skewering him on the inside.

"You couldn't force her to go to the police," Maggie said.

"She's right," Joanne agreed.

They all looked at Sam for confirmation. He was quiet, and then his gaze met Michael's, and he said, "I've tried to help a lot of people over the years, and the one thing I know is, if they don't want the help, you can't force it on them."

"Does her family know?" Michael asked.

"Her only living relative is an aunt in Westerly, Rhode Island," Sam said. "They're going to talk to her today."

The nurse bustled in, and they all went silent.

"I'm sorry, I'm going to need you all to wait outside while we dress his head wound," she said.

Joanne patted Michael's hand. "I'll be right back."

He nodded. His face was set in hard lines, and he looked

as if the weight of world was sitting squarely on his shoulders.

In all the years Maggie had known him, she'd never seen Michael look defeated. He was the sort of guy who, if life handed him lemons, he would shrug and be happy because, hey, free lemons. But now, now he just looked lost, as if everything he'd ever believed about life had proven to be a lie.

The three of them entered the waiting room to find Claire and Ginger there. They quickly enfolded Joanne in hugs, and the three of them took seats in the corner so Joanne could catch them up on all that had happened.

"What happens now?" Maggie asked as she and Sam moved a few feet away from the others.

"I post a guard by Michael's door," he said in a low voice. "I've been having my deputies do extra rounds in and around the hospital, but now I think I'm going to post someone at all times in the ICU."

"Because you think Michael's guilty?" Maggie asked. Her outrage made her voice sharp.

"No," Sam said. "Because I think the killer will be worried that Michael remembers more than he does, and Michael could be a possible target."

"Oh," Maggie said. She hung her head. "I look like a big jerk right now, don't I?"

"Little bit," Sam agreed. When her head snapped up, he smiled. "But I like that you defend your friends so fiercely. It's a very attractive quality."

Maggie smiled at him. "Thank you."

"You're welcome," he said. He leaned forward and kissed her. It was swift and sweet, and when he stepped back he studied her closely. "Promise me that you will not do any more investigating of any kind on this case. We just crossed over into some seriously scary territory."

Maggie opened her mouth to speak, but he cut her off.

"No, I'm serious, Maggie," he said. "This is a real psychopath we're dealing with, and I don't want you in harm's way. Promise me."

"Are you done now?" she asked. "Because I was about to swear that I would steer clear when I was so rudely interrupted."

"Sorry," he said. "I worry."

"Me, too," she said. "So, please, be careful."

Her voice was soft, betraying how truly frightened she was. She couldn't bear the thought of anything happening to Sam. She hugged him close, wanting to imprint the feel of him against her.

"I will," he said, and he hugged back.

But Maggie knew that life didn't work around the promises you made to each other, but rather, it happened and you worked around it, trying to keep those promises intact even when the odds were against you.

At the insistence of the other GBGs and Michael, Joanne went home to take a nap. The bags under her eyes were big enough to pack for a week in Hawaii, and she looked like she was about to drop where she stood. Ginger took her home to tuck her in and make sure she stayed there.

Maggie knew she had left Laura to run the shop much more than she should have, so she spent the afternoon in the store, catching Laura up on what was happening.

"But St. Stanley is so small," Laura said. "Surely, we'd notice if there was a psychotic killer from another state here."

"You'd think," Maggie said. "But it's the holidays, and family and friends are pouring in from out of town, and we can't know them all."

Laura and Maggie were folding a stack of sweaters that they had decided to display in open shelves by the front door during the winter months.

"I suppose," Laura said. "You know, I keep going over every conversation I had with Diane—or rather, Leann—and I just can't believe that I never picked up on any of what she was going through. I thought she was just terminally shy."

"She was probably trying to put it behind her, and you helped with that," Maggie said.

"Maybe." Laura sounded unconvinced. "Or by dragging her out and making her do things, I made her a target."

"What do you mean?"

"What if it isn't some psycho stalker who got her?" Laura glanced up from the sweater in her arms. "What if it was Britney Bergstrom?"

Maggie stopped moving and met her daughter's gaze. "I had the same thought."

"No, really?" Laura asked.

"Well, she was so hateful and threatening in the shop that day," Maggie said. "I meant to mention it to Sam, but I forgot."

"I think you should tell him," Laura said. "And I'll back you up, and Aaron and the others heard how nasty she was at the ball."

"But would she have taken pictures of her?" Maggie asked. "And as far as I know, Britney has never been to Rhode Island."

"That doesn't mean it wasn't Britney," Laura said. "She's always been a hideous bully. Maybe she went to the deli to confront Leann and ended up strangling her."

Laura was twisting the sweater in her hands and Maggie reached forward and freed the cashmere from her grip.

"I'll talk to Sam," she said.

"Oh, thanks," Laura said, shaking out her fingers before she reached for another sweater. She tucked the neck of a sweater under her chin as she folded it into thirds, then placed it on one of the top shelves. "You know, what I don't understand is why she didn't go to the police."

"Michael said she was afraid that the person stalking her was powerful," Maggie said. "It makes no sense to me, but maybe she was afraid it was a police officer."

"But how could that be?" Laura asked. "Unless Sam has a new hire from Rhode Island, how could she think that?"

Maggie stared at her daughter. Did Sam have a new hire? Surely, he would have thought of that himself? She couldn't call him and ask. She would be doing exactly what he'd asked her not to do, prying into the case.

Still, she hadn't told him about Britney. And really, was it butting in to tell him about someone who had threatened the victim? Surely, not. This was just her being a good citizen. Right?

"I have to go make a quick call," she said.

Laura grinned at her, and said, "Good luck."

Maggie blew out a breath. She had a feeling she was going to need it.

Chapter 22

Maggie ducked into her office and used her landline to call Sam's office. She was on the paranoid side, she knew, but she didn't want to use cell phones for this conversation.

He answered on the second ring. "Sheriff Collins speaking."

"Hi, Sam," she said.

"Maggie, are you all right?"

"Fine," she assured him. "Sam, have you hired anyone new lately?"

He was quiet for a moment and then let out a huff of breath that even through the phone Maggie could tell was exasperation.

"Let me guess: You think because Leann was afraid of going to the authorities, I must have hired her killer during the past two months?" he asked.

"You already had this thought, didn't you?" she asked.

"Yes," he said. "And no, I haven't hired anyone. The last hire was under the former sheriff, and it was Stephen Rourke, and I believe he's friends with Ginger's oldest son, Aaron."

Maggie remembered seeing the young man on one of her visits to the station.

"Well, it was just a thought," she said.

"Uh-huh," he said. "I thought you were going to steer clear."

"I am," she said. "That's why I called you instead of coming over to the station to talk to the deputies myself. See? Big improvement."

"I'm impressed," he said, although he didn't really sound it. "Look, I've gotten the records from the electrical company of everyone who has requested new service in St. Stanley over the past two months. If our killer is new to town, hopefully we'll find him on this list."

"Good idea," Maggie said. "Of course, if it's a man, you might want to get a listing of new cable subscribers."

"Already done," he said.

"Wow, now *I'm* impressed," Maggie said.

"Don't be," he said. His frustration with the case was clear in his voice. "At least, not until we make an arrest."

"You'll find him," Maggie said. "I know it, and since we're offering up theories—"

"We are?" he interrupted.

"Do you know Britney Bergstrom?" Maggie forged ahead, ignoring his wry tone.

"No," he said. "Is there a reason I should?"

"No. Well, maybe. She was in my shop the day before the ball, and she wanted the dress that I had already rented to Diane, but I refused to sell it to her. Britney was very verbally abusive about it and threatened Diane in the shop and then again at the ball."

Sam was silent, and Maggie wondered if she had annoyed him. In the old days, back when they were enemies and even when they were trying to be friends, she would have been pleased to get under his skin, but this new relationship status was tricky. She found she didn't like the thought that she had annoyed him, which in and of itself was alarming.

"Are you mad?" she asked.

"No," he said. "Well, not at you at any rate. This case is just making me rip my hair out. No clues. No evidence. And every time I think I might have a hold on what happened, it slips through my fingers like smoke."

Maggie could feel his frustration pulsing through the phone. She did not envy him his task.

"Maybe you could flush the killer out by having a memorial service for her," Maggie said.

"Again, what part of *stop thinking about this case* do you not understand?" he asked.

"Just hear me out," Maggie said. She began to pace around her tiny office, but it was too crowded, so she moved into her storage area. "I know it's a very TV-sitcom idea, but isn't there psychological evidence that shows killers are likely to show up at their victims' funerals?"

"There is a theory that serial killers like to attend the funerals of their victims so they can relive the moment of their ultimate power, but we have no evidence that whoever killed Leann Winthrop was a serial killer, and if your suggestion that it was Britney Bergstrom over a dress is true, then I sincerely doubt she'll be showing up at the funeral."

"Even so, there should be a service for Leann," Maggie said. She glanced out at her shop and noted the holiday decorations.

Leann wasn't going to be celebrating this holiday or any others. It suddenly struck Maggie that even though she was new to St. Stanley, Leann deserved a decent memorial service.

"Just think about it," she said.

"Why?" Sam asked. "You already have it half planned in your head."

"I'll keep it simple," she said. "Do you think her aunt would like to come?"

"She's elderly and lives in an assisted-care facility. She's not capable of making such a long trip," Sam said. "I think she's planning to have a service when Leann's remains are returned to her."

Maggie felt her throat get tight. She didn't know the aunt at all, and she had barely known Leann. Still, to lose a loved one in such a tragic and horrible way—it was a crushing blow.

"I'll talk to Laura and see what she thinks of the idea," Maggie said.

"And the Claramottas," Sam said. "Joanne and Michael may have some strong feelings about this."

"Of course," Maggie agreed.

"Call me tonight," Sam said. It wasn't a question. Maggie understood that he was going to trust her to take this over and manage it.

"Thanks, Sam," she said.

"We'll talk more later," he said.

As she hung up the phone, Maggie realized she liked the sound of that.

The service was held two days later in the small Congregational church just off the town green. Leann had attended the Sunday service there a couple of times during her time in St. Stanley, so Maggie felt that it was appropriate. Reverend White officiated the modest service, and Laura did a reading about the power of a friendship that had ended too soon.

Surprisingly, the little white church with the spire was packed to bursting. Maggie didn't know if it was idle curiosity, empathy for the tragedy of a slain young woman just a few days before Christmas or Ginger Lancaster's pound cakes and Alice Franklin's pies that had brought in the hordes of mourners.

She and Sam sat behind Michael, Joanne and Doc Franklin. Although he was still weak, Michael had insisted upon attending. Dr. Graber had not been happy and had only agreed to let him leave the hospital if Doc Franklin was with him at all times.

The rest of the staff from the deli sat with him, and Maggie looked each of them over. She knew Sam had already checked them for alibis and to be certain that Michael hadn't hired anyone new who might have followed Leann to St. Stanley. Leann had been his only recent hire over the past year.

A wreath of simple white roses and a framed picture of Leann from the Madison ball stood on a small table in front of the pulpit. To Maggie it felt as if so little had been left behind to mark the life of such a lovely young woman. A surge of anger rocketed through her and she squeezed Sam's hand.

She heard him hiss in a breath, and asked, "Did you see someone?"

Maggie loosened her grip. "No, I just felt a surge of hot-damn mad. Sorry."

Sam rubbed her thumb with his in a soothing gesture. "It's okay. I get it."

Maggie imagined that he did. How he'd spent his entire career working cases like this, she had no idea. How did one separate his emotions from watching innocent people suffer at the hands of others? She didn't think she could do it.

"It isn't easy," Sam said. "You learn to compartmentalize, or the anger starts to eat at you."

She wondered how he'd read her mind, but then she supposed it wasn't that hard to imagine what she'd been thinking. She glanced past him toward the other side of the church. It would be so helpful if Leann's murderer were wearing a sign around his neck that said he'd strangled her, but of course no one was.

From what she could see, the crowd was made up of St. Stanley regulars. People who worked hard to keep roofs over their families' heads, paid their taxes, took annual summer trips to the shore and tried to do the right thing even when it was the hardest thing to do.

"I don't see anyone here who could be the killer, do you?" Maggie asked.

"No," Sam shook his head. He sounded as frustrated as she felt, and Maggie squeezed his hand again, but gently this time, to let him know that she understood.

It was impossible for her to imagine that one of these people had killed Leann. Her eyes flitted over Summer Phillips where she sat with Tyler Fawkes. Yes, even Summer seemed an unlikely candidate, as much as Maggie would have liked it to be otherwise.

There just wasn't any point to it. None of these people were from the northeast, and what reason could they have had to harm Leann? Unless, of course, there was a psychopath living among them who had heard that Leann had a stalker and decided to reenact the whole scene by becoming her new stalker.

Maggie felt a chill rush over her skin. Was that possible? Could it be that someone had discovered that Leann was hiding out and, knowing that they had a victim in their midst, had killed her?

"What is it?" Sam asked. "Your entire body just went tense. Did you see someone?"

Maggie forced herself to relax. "No, I just had a crazy thought."

"Do tell," Sam said.

They were whispering, but Maggie didn't want to take away from the service, which was wrapping up, nor did she want to bring any attention to herself or Sam.

"I'll tell you after," she said. She turned and glanced at him, and he gave her a nod of understanding.

There was a small reception after the service in the hall attached to the sanctuary. Maggie used the big urn for coffee while Ginger made another for water for tea. The December afternoon was brisk, and she knew the hot beverages would be welcome before everyone went back out into the cold. Together Maggie and Ginger worked the table, handing out cups and plates and exchanging words with the people they had known most of their lives.

Several people came up to Laura to compliment her eulogy. Maggie watched her daughter handle the kind words with humility and grace. She knew Leann's murder had been a shock for Laura, and she was impressed that the little girl who had once spent an afternoon sobbing over a squashed ladybug had the poise to speak in front of a crowd about the horrifying loss of her new friend.

Maggie had gotten up the other night and found Laura sitting on the sunporch in her bathrobe and slippers. Silent tears had been streaming down her face, and Maggie had sat beside her and put her arm about her. They had sat like that for a long time.

They hadn't spoken of what was wrong. They both knew, and there was no point, since words could not heal the pain Laura was feeling. But they'd taken comfort in each other's nearness, and that had been enough.

Maggie hated that her daughter had to have another loss in her life. She'd already buried her father and his parents, and a few pets had come and gone, but this was the first time Laura had lost someone her own age, someone who shouldn't be gone except for the fact that she'd somehow garnered the attention of a killer.

A shiver rippled through Maggie, and Ginger glanced up from the table where she was slicing up another cake.

"Are you all right?"

"Yeah, I just had a ghost walk over my grave," she said. Ginger gave her a sharp look.

"Figure of speech," Maggie said. "Sorry."

"No, it's all right. This whole thing just has me as twitchy as a squirrel," Ginger said. She glanced across the room, where her son Aaron was standing with Laura and Blake, Max and Bianca. "She wasn't much older than them. She had her whole life ahead of her. It just breaks my heart."

"So, are you going to tell me your theory now?" Sam asked as he joined them.

"Well, it's probably stupid," Maggie said. "But I was thinking that we're looking for a stranger, someone from Rhode Island or somewhere in the northeast, who would stick out in St. Stanley, right?"

"Yeah," Sam said. "It does appear that she was pursued down the coast by her original stalker."

"What if she wasn't?"

"I'm not following."

Both Ginger and Sam gave Maggie perplexed looks while she paused to fill up a plate with cream-cheese cookies for Mrs. Shoemaker.

"Okay, I know this sounds crazy, but what if someone knew she was being harassed? What if they knew it and they used it to make it look like the killer had gotten her?"

"You mean the real stalker didn't get her but a copycat did?" Ginger asked. "You're right. That is nuts."

"But why would he do that?" Sam asked. Maggie was heartened that he hadn't dismissed her idea as whacko as fast as Ginger had.

"Maybe he's a budding psychopath or he had a vendetta against Michael or he planned to rob the place and using a stalking situation worked for him," Maggie said. "I don't know. The point is, who exactly knew that Leann was hiding out here?"

Sam put a hand on the back of his neck. "It's worth checking out, assuming that we can get a line on anyone who knew Leann's backstory."

"I still think it's reaching," Ginger said. "I mean, if that's true, then what you're saying is that it's one of our own."

Maggie didn't like it, either, but when she studied the room, she noted that the two most likely suspects were still Michael and Joanne, and she knew it wasn't either of them. So, it had to be someone else here. It just had to be.

"Hi, everyone," Claire said as she approached the group. "It was a very nice service, Maggie."

"Thanks," Maggie said.

"So, did you see anyone who looked suspicious?" Claire asked Sam.

He shook his head. "It was a long shot."

Claire blew out a breath and gave Sam a considering look.

"I don't want to sound paranoid," she said, "but there's been a man coming to the library for the past three mornings. He's in his late twenties and looks like he has a job, but he doesn't talk to anyone. He comes in right when we open and sits in a corner by the window and reads the paper, and then he leaves for the day. I'm sure he's probably harmless, but since Leann's killer is assumed to be a stranger and he's the only one I've seen, I just thought . . ."

Her voice trailed off, and Sam nodded at her.

"I'll check it out," he said. "Thanks, Claire. That's exactly the kind of information we need."

"Doc Franklin says it's time to take Michael home or he's threatening to call Dr. Graber at the hospital and have Michael readmitted," Joanne said as she joined them. "Thanks for doing this, Maggie. I think it helped Michael a little."

"I hope so," Maggie said. "It's a terrible burden he's put on himself."

"If you want, I can come and talk to him later," Sam offered. "I know a little bit about how he's feeling."

"Oh, Sam, that would be nice," Joanne said. "I keep telling him that it's not his fault, but he doesn't hear me. It'd be better coming from you."

"I'll be over after my shift," Sam promised.

Joanne left to take Michael home, and Maggie promised to check on her later.

Others came over to the group to say good-bye, and although Maggie hadn't intended to be Leann's representative, she realized that by being the organizer of the service, she was by default the person who everyone felt the need to thank.

The realization made her sad. It was yet more evidence that Leann had really been alone in the world. When Maggie rested her gaze on Laura and Sandy and the GBGs, she couldn't help but feel so very lucky to have them all in her life.

"Hey, Mom, I'm going to go for coffee with some friends," Laura said as she stopped by the table. Her eyes were swollen and the tip of her nose was pink. It was clear she had been crying.

Maggie opened her arms, and Laura stepped into them. It was a fierce, bolstering hug that Maggie gave her, and Laura looked a little better when she stepped back.

"You gave a wonderful eulogy," Maggie said.

"It really was," Sam chimed in.

"Thanks," Laura said. She looked watery again. "I just wish I hadn't had to, you know?"

Sam and Maggie both nodded. They watched her walk away, and Maggie felt her chest get tight. She hated that Laura had been exposed to such evil, and yet she knew that she couldn't shelter her from life's horrors no matter how much she wished she could.

Sam looped an arm around her and pulled her close, as if sensing her distress. Maggie leaned against him, grateful for his strength.

"Psst," Claire hissed at them from a few feet away. "Psst."

Both Sam and Maggie turned to look at her. Her eyes were round, and she crooked one finger and pointed in the direction of the door.

"That's him," she whispered. "The strange man I told you about."

Chapter 23

Maggie felt Sam straighten up beside her. She peered over at a young man dressed in khakis and a crisp blue shirt under a tailored black leather jacket. The jacket hung on him like he wore it loose on purpose. Maggie's first thought was that maybe he was concealing weapons of some sort.

His hair was an unremarkable shade of brown, and he wore glasses, making the color of his eyes hard to discern from across the room, but Maggie suspected that, like his hair, they were also brown.

He stood with his back to the wall, studying everyone in the room with a thorough gaze that made Maggie think he didn't miss much.

He seemed particularly interested in the people who were still milling about, probably angling for seconds of Ginger's pound cake.

The man's gaze scanned the room as if he was looking

for someone. Despite his youth, he had a world-weary look in his eyes that reminded Maggie of Sam. It was as if he'd witnessed too much inhumanity and was no longer surprised by anything but kindness. She knew it was just an instinct, but she had a hard time picturing him as a murderer.

"Excuse me," Sam said. He left Maggie's side and strode with purpose toward the man.

The man seemed to sense Sam coming immediately. He pushed off the wall and turned on his heel, heading for the nearest exit. Sam picked up his pace, and the man did, too.

"Oh my," Claire whispered. "I think he's running away."

"Maybe he's the murderer," Ginger said.

They watched in stunned silence as the man broke into a run. Sam shouted at him to stop, but he was disregarded as the man kicked it into higher gear. He knocked a bunch of chairs over behind him, slowing Sam down, as he had to leap over them.

The remaining guests stood speechlessly watching as the young man slammed into the exit. He was going to get away. Before it was a fully formed thought, Maggie was sprinting across the room to the other exit, planning to block the man from running around the building and back to the parking lot.

She flew out the door, and the cold air hit her like a slap. She didn't slow down and reached the corner of the building just in time to hear a man yelp and the other door—the door Sam had been headed toward—slam open.

Standing with one wedge-heel shoe planted firmly on the runner's chest and pointing her stun gun at him like she'd be more than happy to zap him, was Deputy Dot Wilson.

"You made me get mud on my new TOMS," Dot said as

she wagged her foot in his face. "I ought to blast you just for that."

The man looked at her with wide eyes behind his glasses as if afraid she really would use her Taser in a fit of pique.

"Good timing, Deputy Wilson," Sam said.

"Yeah, nice one," Maggie agreed.

Sam turned and glared at her, and Maggie frowned when she realized he wasn't breathing hard at all, while she was sucking air in and out like the bellows for a fireplace.

"There's been a mistake," the man said, but Dot interrupted him.

"Hush," she said. "I just came to pay my respects." She waved a hand to indicate the formfitting navy dress she was wearing.

"Very nice," Sam said.

Dot gave him an appreciative nod, and continued, "Then I heard you shout, and this fool came flying out the door like his backside was on fire. I figured something was going down."

"It is. Cover me," Sam said.

He yanked the man up to his feet and pushed him against the wall, where he patted him down. The search revealed a gun in a shoulder holster and a knife strapped to his ankle.

"You have a permit?" Sam asked.

"Yes," the man said. "Look, you're the sheriff, right?"

"That's what the badge says."

"I'm a private investigator," the man said. "Let me get my wallet. You can see my ID."

Sam looked suspicious, but he let the man retrieve his wallet and hand it to him. He passed off the man's gun and knife to Dot while he studied his license.

Josie Belle

"Joel Lipscomb," Sam read his name off of his license. "You're from Rhode Island?"

Joel nodded.

"You're going to have to come down to the station with me," Sam said.

"I'm not the stalker," Joel said. "I was hired by Marjorie Winthrop to find her grandniece's killer."

"Is that so?" Sam asked.

"I was going to introduce myself to you, but I wanted to get a feel for the place first," Joel said.

"You've been here for three days," Sam said. "Were you planning on hanging up curtains before you stopped by?"

Joel's eyebrows lifted behind his glasses. "You're well informed."

"It's my town," Sam said.

Maggie and Dot glanced back and forth between them, watching the verbal volleyball.

"Okay," Joel said. He held out his hand. "Can I have my equipment back?"

"I think I'll just hang on to it for you until we get back to my office," Sam said. "Need a lift?"

"Thanks, but I know where it is," Joel said.

"Yeah, but I'd feel better if you stayed in my sight," Sam said. "You understand."

Joel gave him a chagrinned nod, and Maggie knew he understood that, as far as Sam was concerned, he was a person of interest.

"Maggie, I'll call you later," Sam said.

Ginger and Claire came outside and joined her and Dot as they watched the two men drive away.

"A private eye named Joel," Dot said. She shook her head. "I thought they were supposed to have cool names like Philip, Mike or Rex."

"Only fictionally," Maggie said.

"Well, there goes my great lead," Claire said. "I never would have pegged him for a private eye. Do you think he's legit?"

"Yes," Maggie said. "Otherwise he would have been riding in the back of Sam's car."

"Ah," Claire said. "He's the only stranger I've seen in town other than visiting family. If the killer's not him, then who?"

Ginger and Maggie exchanged a glance, and Ginger rolled her eyes.

"No, I still don't believe it," Ginger said. "It doesn't make sense. Other than Summer Phillips, who do we know in town who fits the profile of a psychopath?"

"Believe what?" Claire asked, looking confused.

"Maggie thinks that someone in town knew that Leann was being stalked, and he used the information to kill her and let her original stalker be blamed."

"It was just a theory," Maggie protested. "But you have to admit it's possible."

"Well sure, anything is possible," Ginger said. "But that doesn't make it likely."

They were interrupted by the last of the stragglers, who had finally left the reception hall and were making their way to their cars.

The three of them spent the next hour cleaning up so as not to leave a mess for the church ladies who had been so kind to let them use their reception room. When they were finished, Maggie walked over to the office and turned in the key to the room.

Mrs. Diaz, who worked in the church office, took the keys and gave Maggie a warm smile. "I popped my head in, and it seemed like a really nice service."

"Reverend White was wonderful," Maggie said. "Please thank him for me."

"I will," she promised. "You take care now."

Maggie shut the door behind her. The sky was gray and cold, and the wind had a bitter nip to it. She wondered if they'd have a freeze warning tonight. She wanted to hurry back to the shop, since she and Laura had agreed to close for the memorial. Although she had made a nice chunk of change for the Madison ball, she knew that the holidays were days away, and she wanted to be open as much as possible to get the last-minute holiday shoppers.

Yesterday, she had checked her supply of wrapping paper and noticed that it was running low. She decided to stop by Janice's stationery store and pick up some more before returning to the shop. She really hoped the sale was still going. It killed her to think of paying full price. She had to remember to pick up loads of paper just after the holidays for next year.

Ginger and Claire had both gone back to work, so Maggie parked her car by her shop and trudged through the center of town on her own, burrowing into her jacket and snapping up her collar to keep the icy fingers of winter away from her skin.

She pulled open the door to Write On. It was abuzz with holiday shoppers. Carols played softly in the background and, if it had been any other day, Maggie would have felt cheered. Instead, she was again reminded of Leann and how she wouldn't be celebrating this Christmas or any others.

She headed over to where she knew the wrapping paper was. Last year's good stuff had been thoroughly picked over by her crew, and the remaining paper didn't wow her. She glanced around the shop, looking for Janice. She thought maybe if she bought in bulk, she could wrangle a deal for the good stuff.

She found Janice helping Donna Schwartz with a gift for her grandson's bar mitzvah. Janice had an excellent selection of specialty cards to cover any occasion.

"This will do nicely," Donna said. "Thank you, dear."

"You're welcome, and congratulations," Janice said. "You must be very proud."

"I am, but oh, where has the time gone?" Donna asked. "How is it that my bubele is now a young man?"

Janice smiled in understanding, and Maggie nodded. She knew exactly how Donna felt. It seemed like just yesterday that Laura was a dimple-kneed toddler, and now she was giving eloquent eulogies. It was enough to give a mother whiplash.

As Donna went to the cash register to pay, Janice turned to Maggie. "What can I do for you, Maggie?"

"I'm looking to broker a deal," she said.

Janice's eyebrows lifted. "Really?"

"I'm almost out of wrapping paper," Maggie said. "And I was wondering, if I buy in bulk, would you cut me a deal?"

"Hmm." Janice tapped her chin with her finger while she pondered the question. "I suppose it would depend upon how much you were willing to purchase."

"You don't want to get stuck with as much as you did last Christmas," Maggie said. "Then you have to store it, and it takes up too much room, and it's out of fashion for next year."

"Uh-huh, and then I'd have to have a sale, where the local thrift-store owners get into a brawl over it," Janice added. She winked at Maggie, letting her know she was just kidding.

"Yeah, that sort of thing," Maggie said.

Janice led her over to the new-paper display. Next to it was an array of small gifts, from candles to picture frames. Maggie had a feeling this section catered to the man who has no idea what to buy his mother, wife, sister or female friend. Grab a picture frame, a candle and a gift bag and *wham!* Shopping done.

"Very clever to group complementary items in one area for the shopping impaired," Maggie said.

Janice grinned. "I haven't been in business for twenty years for nothing. Let me check my stock in back and see if we can do a deal."

"Sure," Maggie said. "It'll give me a chance to do some holiday shopping of my own."

Janice left, and Maggie turned to the gift display. She had pretty much figured out what she was giving everyone on her list. The only one left was Sam. What was she supposed to get him? Was she supposed to get him anything at all? She'd feel like a complete boob if she bought him something and he didn't think they were there yet.

Then again, what if he bought her something really nice? Ack. She could feel her insides twist with anxiety. She thought she might have to ask Ginger to tell Roger to have a chat with Sam and see what he could find out. Men were hopeless at that sort of thing, but she was pretty sure Ginger could coach Roger into getting the information out of Sam.

She checked out the frames, and saw a pewter frame that was stamped with MEOW and had fish skeletons scattered all around it. If she could just get a picture of Sam's cat, Marshall Dillon, it would make a thoughtful but not sickening gift.

Maggie picked up the frame and turned it over to see the price. It was on the high side, in her opinion, but she figured if Janice had this area set up for the desperate, she could charge pretty steep prices even for picture frames. She'd have to think about it.

She put the frame back, and her attention was caught by another frame. Made of thick wood that was painted cream white with gold trim, it contained a small, wallet-size photo of a pretty young woman. The model looked familiar, and Maggie frowned as she tried to place her.

Was she a celebrity? Maggie didn't think so, but she was sure she had seen a photo of this girl before, looking off to the right with the wind blowing her hair about her face as she stood in front of the beach.

She picked up the frame and turned it over. She was too puzzled to feel any sticker shock this time.

"That's one of my most popular frames," Janice said as she came to stand beside Maggie. "I just sold the last one a few weeks ago, but a new shipment came in today, so I put some out."

"Is the girl in this famous?" Maggie asked. "She seems familiar."

"I don't think so," Janice frowned. "As far as I know, it's

just a stock photo. Men seem to like her. I sell more of this frame to men than any other. At least, I sold the last one to a young man. He seemed quite taken with the photo."

"A young man in his twenties?" Maggie asked. She felt the blood rush into her ears, and her heart slowed to an ominous pounding that made breathing difficult.

"Yes, why?" Janice asked. "Maggie, are you all right? You don't look so good."

"Was he wearing a camel-colored overcoat?" Maggie asked.

"Yes, yes, he was," she said.

"Janice, I need this picture," Maggie said. "It's imperative."

"I don't understand," Janice said.

"I think this picture will lead us to Leann Winthrop's killer," Maggie said.

Janice blinked at her and took the frame from her hands. She managed to loosen the back of the frame with just her fingernails and took the picture out.

"You'll explain this to me later?" she asked as she handed the photo to Maggie.

"I promise."

Maggie took the photo and carefully put it in her purse. She glanced at her phone to check the time. With any luck, Sam would still be at the station talking to PI Joel.

"Thanks, Janice," she called as she dashed out the door and into the street.

She'd recognized the photo in her purse, not because the model was famous, but because it had been shown to her before. Blake Caulfield, on the day she had met him, had shown her the picture of his fiancée, a picture he'd kept in his wallet.

Except now Maggie knew that she wasn't his fiancée. She was just a picture he'd taken out of a frame to pretend he had a fiancée. The question was why? But then it was obvious, wasn't it? Having a photo that he showed around as his fiancée made him look innocent of his real intent, didn't it?

Maggie fumbled with her phone. She needed to call Laura and tell her to stay away from Blake until they knew what was going on. Several people called greetings to her as she ran toward the station and used her phone at the same time. Laura didn't answer, so Maggie paused and sent her a quick text. She didn't want to write anything that Blake might read while he was with her, so she kept it simple.

Need to talk to you about Sam. Call me as soon as you get this.

Maggie knew that the message would be irresistible to Laura and yet would give nothing away.

She hurried into the station to see that Deputy Wilson was back and working the front counter.

"Hello, Maggie." Dot greeted her with a warm smile, which quickly faded as she took in Maggie's face. "What's wrong?"

"I need to speak to Sam," Maggie said. "I think I know who murdered Leann Winthrop."

Chapter 24

Dot moved with a swiftness that belied her stocky build. She snapped up the counter that led to the back offices and gestured for Maggie to come through.

Maggie followed Dot into the back. Dot paused to rap on a closed wooden door.

"Sheriff, Maggie is here to see you," Dot said.

"Come in," Sam said without any hesitation.

Dot pushed open the door, and they saw Sam and Joel. Both men were standing, examining several crime-scene pictures that were spread across the top of the desk. Maggie didn't look. She'd seen it live and really didn't want to relive the grisly memory.

"What is it, Maggie?" Sam asked. His eyes narrowed as he took in her expression, and Maggie wondered if she looked as shell-shocked as she felt.

She fished in her purse for the picture she'd found at the

stationery store. She took it out of her bag with shaking fingers and handed it to Sam. He glanced at the small, wallet-size photo and then at her, clearly not understanding the relevance, but how could he have?

"This picture came from a frame in Janice's shop," Maggie said. "I recognized it because Blake Caulfield showed me the same photo a few weeks ago and told me it was his fiancée, but obviously she's not. It was just a stock picture from a frame he'd bought at Janice's. She remembered him. So, his whole story about a fiancée is a lie. But why would he lie unless he has something to hide, like the fact that he is Leann's stalker and murderer?"

"Isn't Caulfield the guy Laura has been spending so much time with?" Sam asked.

Maggie nodded. She could feel the panic thumping through her. She checked her phone, but there had been no incoming messages or calls. Why hadn't Laura returned her text?

"Maggie, I know it looks bad, but there could be another explanation," Sam said. "What do we know about Blake?"

"He bought the Anne Barge dress that's in the window of my shop," she said. "He told me it was for his fiancée, but then he returned it, saying she'd broken things off with him."

"When, Maggie? When did he return it?" Sam asked. His voice took on an intensity that made Maggie's skin prickle.

"I don't know. . . . Wait." She tried to picture when it had happened, and her stomach dropped to her feet. It was hard to speak around her throat, which had suddenly gone dry. "I was in the hospital with Joanne when Laura called to tell me he had returned it. It was after Leann's murder."

Sam reached out to her as if he thought she might faint. Maggie looked at him, and she knew her terror was in her voice when she said, "I texted Laura, but she hasn't answered."

"How did he pay for the gown?" Joel asked. "If it was a credit card transaction, we could try to trace him that way."

"It was cash," Maggie said. She felt woozy. "He even made a joke about how he hadn't planned to blow his whole shopping budget on one gift. Oh, god, I thought he was being romantic."

"What did Laura tell you the last time you spoke with her?" Sam asked.

Maggie started to pace. What had Laura said exactly?

"It was when she was leaving the reception," Maggie said. "She said she was going for coffee with friends."

"That could include Max and Bianca or Aaron, right?" Sam asked. He pulled out his phone. "I'll call Max."

"Yes, she definitely said *friends* plural," Maggie said. She took out her phone, too, and called Bianca.

Both Joel and Dot stood quietly watching them as Maggie and Sam talked.

"Max, it's Sam. Have you seen Laura?" Sam asked.

"Bianca, it's Maggie. Is Laura with you?" Maggie said a second later. She was trying to listen to Sam's conversation and have her own at the same time.

"No," Bianca answered. "We were at the Daily Grind together, but she and Blake left a while ago."

"Where did they go?" Maggie asked.

"When did they leave?" Sam asked.

"A half an hour ago, maybe more," Bianca said. "Maggie, you sound funny. Is everything okay?"

Maggie glanced at Sam. She didn't know how much to say, so she listened as he said, "If you see or hear from Laura, tell her to get in touch immediately. And if you see or hear from Blake Caulfield, let me know. It's important. No, I can't go into the details right now."

Maggie repeated what Sam said and then ended her call. She looked at Sam, and asked, "Now what?"

"Now we find Laura," he said. "Does she have your car? What does Caulfield's car look like?"

"My car is at my shop," Maggie said. "I only saw Blake's car once, at night, when he picked Laura up to go see a band at the Daily Grind. It was a generic silver sedan."

"Does Laura have a GPS app on her phone?" Joel asked.

"Not that I know of," Maggie said. "But I don't know half of what she has on there. Why?"

"That would be the easiest way to track her," Joel said. "Give me all the info you know about her phone, and I'll see what I can do."

While Joel turned his attention to Sam's computer, Dot and Maggie each began calling around town to anyone who might have seen Laura. Maggie started with Sandy and Jake in case Laura had gone home. She hadn't. Sandy and Jake packed Josh into his car seat and went looking for her. Then she called the Good Buy Girls. No one had seen her. Ginger put Roger and her boys on high alert, and Roger and Aaron went out looking for her. Claire let everyone at the library know to be on the lookout, and Joanne started calling around to the stores that Laura was known to frequent to see if she was shopping for gifts.

Sam radioed all of the deputies who were on duty and let them know to be on the lookout for Laura, and then he called in all of the deputies who were off duty and told them to pick up cars at the station and start searching.

Joel worked away on Sam's office computer to see if he could track her through the cell phone information Maggie had just given him.

As Maggie ended her call with Joanne, she tried to find comfort in the flurry of activity around her, but the reality was that Laura was a type-A personality. She got top marks in school, she was never late, she always said please and thank you and she always answered her phone, especially if it was Maggie calling.

Down in the deepest part of herself, Maggie knew that Laura was in trouble. She could feel her insides fracturing from the weight of the terror that was crushing her, but she knew she couldn't give in to it. She had to stay strong; she had to think; she had to find her daughter.

As everyone finished their calls, only the clicking of the computer keys under Joel's fingers broke the silence of the room.

"How's it going, Joel?" Sam asked.

"It'll take time," he said. "I'm going to use the SS7 public switched network routes to try to pinpoint the location of her cell phone number. It includes the home location register, which cellular networks use to determine phone location."

"In English?" Sam asked.

"I'm piggybacking onto other networks and searching for her," he said.

"How do you have access to this information?" Sam asked. "Never mind. I'm not sure I want to know."

Joel gave him a shifty glance. "Let's just leave it at 'I'm a computer geek.'"

"If you ever have a hankering to be a deputy in Virginia . . ." Sam began, and Joel interrupted, "I'll let you know."

The sound of voices came from the lobby, and Dot ducked out to see what was happening.

"Maggie," her voice said over the intercom a moment later, "you've got people here."

Maggie hurried out to the front. Claire and Ginger stood there, looking wide-eyed and worried. Maggie went right into their arms. What little strength she had in reserve was slipping away from her like sand through an hourglass with every minute that Laura was unaccounted for.

"Any sign of her yet?" Claire asked.

"None," Maggie said.

Sam stepped out of his office, shrugging on his jacket as he went.

"I'm going out to look for her," he said. "I want you to stay here."

"No!" Maggie protested. "I have to go, too. I have to try to find her."

"I can't let you do that," Sam said.

"I'm sorry, but I don't think you have a heck of a lot to say about it," Maggie said. All of her fear was rapidly boiling into misdirected rage. This was her daughter, and she would do whatever it took to find her.

"I got it!" Joel hurried into the main part of the station with a printout in his hand. "Her phone is showing a location off River Road. It looks like an industrial building."

"The abandoned wire factory," Sam and Maggie said together.

Maggie made for the door, but Sam grabbed her elbow.

"Let me go!" she snapped as she tried to jerk free.

"Maggie, no!" Sam's voice was fierce. "You can't go."

"She's my baby, Sam," she protested.

"And if you go barging in there, you'll likely get her killed," he said.

Maggie stilled. That was the last thing she wanted. Sam cupped her face and forced her to meet his gaze.

"This is my job. This is what I do," he said. "I'll get Laura for you, but you have to stay here . . . because I love you, Maggie, and I can't do my job if I'm worried about you."

His blue eyes were steady, and Maggie felt her breath catch. She took a deep breath. Laura was the most precious thing in the world to her, and she knew if anyone was going to be able to get her home safely, it was Sam. Still, she felt it was the biggest leap of faith she'd ever taken when she said, "Go get our girl."

Sam gave her a swift kiss and strode out the door, calling to Joel after him, "Come on."

"Mind the phones for me," Dot called as she followed them out.

The station was alarmingly quiet after their departure, and Maggie shivered. She was cold all the way to her bones, and she knew it wasn't from the temperature in the toasty-warm building. She started to straighten the flyers on the bulletin board.

It was a haphazard collection of notices about everything from the curfew ordinance for teens to picking up after your dog. Each flyer was layered over another, rendering the entire board useless.

She began pulling flyers off and soon Ginger and Claire joined her. In minutes the entire bulletin board had been denuded. Maggie stared at the plain brown board. Her insides felt equally as barren.

There was a crackle and squawk on the radio as the other deputies radioed in that they were on their way. It made her jump, and she noticed that Claire and Ginger were equally tense.

She wanted to yell and scream and rip at her hair, but she knew that if she lost it, she might never regain control, so instead, she sifted through the flyers, sorting out the older ones, which had been superseded by newer ones.

Wordlessly, Claire gathered all of the thumbtacks while Ginger continued with the sorting. As Ginger handed her each notice, Maggie took thumbtacks from Claire and fastened the papers so that each was visible by pushing the thumbtacks into the corkboard. Feeling the points stab into the board was satisfying, and the repetitive busywork kept her from having a complete mental collapse. All too soon the board was done, the older papers recycled and the station house quiet.

When the phone rang, the three of them started, and Maggie swallowed hard. This could be very good or very bad. Either way, she had to know.

She snatched up the receiver and said, "Sam."

"I've got her, and she's fine," he said.

A sob of relief gushed out of Maggie in a guttural noise that made both Claire and Ginger step forward as if to brace her.

"Thank you, Sam." Maggie was full-on crying now, and she looked at the others, and said, "She's okay."

Ginger and Claire let out whoops of joy and hugged each other.

"Mom." A voice came on the phone, and Maggie pressed it close to her ear.

"Hi, baby," she said. "Are you all right?"

"Well, I'm here," Laura said. Her voice was shaky. "And up until fifteen minutes ago, I wasn't sure I would be, so, yeah, I'm good."

"Oh, honey," Maggie said. She wanted to hug her daughter so badly she ached with the need.

"It was Blake, Mom," Laura said. Her voice cracked, and Maggie could tell she was sobbing.

"I know, baby," Maggie said. "But it's all right. He can't hurt you now."

"I love you, Mom," Laura said.

"I love you, too," Maggie said.

She heard a low voice in the background, and Laura said, "Sam wants the EMTs to look me over."

"That's probably a good idea."

"I'll see you in a little bit."

"I'll be here."

Maggie closed her eyes, trying to regroup as a riot of emotions coursed through her, leaving her insides as wrecked as if they'd been caught in the path of a hurricane.

"Maggie, listen." Sam was back on the phone now. "We didn't find Blake. I don't know if he heard us coming and split or what."

"Oh no," Maggie said. "You don't think he'll come after Laura again, do you?"

"I don't know. For now I'm keeping her with me, and I'm sending an extra deputy over to the Claramottas," he said.

"Are they—?" Maggie began, but Sam interrupted.

"They're fine, but I want to be cautious until we apprehend Caulfield. He may be afraid that Michael will remember him and try to get rid of him. We're going to have to be very careful. Speaking of which, I want you to stay at the station."

"But Laura," Maggie said. "I need to see her."

"I know, and I'm going to bring her to you as soon as she's been checked out," he said.

"Thank you, Sam," Maggie said. It felt like too little to say to the man who had saved her daughter. And she realized that, while he had told her how he felt about her, she had been too consumed with fear for her daughter to respond. She needed to tell him now. "Sam, about what you said earlier—"

"It's all right, Maggie," he said, interrupting her. "I know it was premature for me to say anything. We can just blame it on the heat of the moment or something."

"Or something," she agreed. "Or I could screw up the courage to tell you that I love you, too."

She saw Claire and Ginger exchange grins, and she felt one part her lips as well.

"Aw, Maggie," Sam said, his voice was rough. "I'm going to kiss you senseless the minute I see you."

Maggie laughed. "Well, get back here quick, then."

"Will do," Sam said, and he ended the call.

Maggie hung up the phone and was immediately embraced by Ginger.

"In the words of my boys," Ginger said, "that was epic."

Claire was next with a hug and a pat on the back.

"I had a feeling about you two," she said.

"It's not all good news," Maggie said. "They found Laura and she was unharmed, but they didn't catch Blake."

Claire frowned. "Do you think he heard them coming and bailed?"

"I don't know," Maggie said. "Sam doesn't either."

"What about Michael?" Ginger asked. "Do they think he's going to go after him?"

"Sam already thought of that and sent an extra deputy over there," Maggie said. "He talked to them and they're fine, but I know he's worried that Caulfield got away."

"I wonder if he'll leave town," Ginger said. "Any sane criminal would."

"Sadly, there's not much evidence that he's sane," Maggie said. "Look what he did to Leann and how easily he fooled us all."

"And how," Ginger agreed. "I actually encouraged my boys to befriend him."

"They say one in four people is a sociopath," Claire said. Maggie and Ginger both looked at her. "What? I read it in a book."

"I never thought I'd say this, but I think you read too much," Maggie said.

Claire smiled, but Ginger frowned.

"I was just kidding," Maggie said.

"No, it's not you," Ginger said. "I thought I heard something. Did either of you hear that?"

They were clustered around the front desk, having not moved away from the phone.

"Hear what?" Claire said.

It was then that Maggie noted how eerily quiet the station was without the radio squawking or the phone ringing. In the early evening darkness, the shadows made by the dim lighting seemed thicker and more ominous.

Maggie felt her heart start to beat hard, and the hair on the back of her neck prickled. She and Ginger exchanged a glance, and she knew her friend felt it, too.

"I don't want to sound paranoid," Ginger said. "But I think there is someone in here with us."

And there it was, the sound of someone coming toward them out of the darkness.

Chapter 25

"Who's there?" Maggie called out.

She saw Claire start beside her, and Ginger turned and scanned the opposite direction. A panicked image of the lush and lithe *Charlie's Angels* girls filled Maggie's head, and she noted that the three of them looked nothing like that. The thought almost made her smile, but then the sound started again.

She strained her ears and noted that it wasn't the sound of footsteps coming toward them; it was more like a scratching noise.

"It's coming from the back, near Sam's office," Maggie said.

"Let's get out of here," Claire said. "Now, while we have the chance."

"But—" Maggie protested.

"No," Ginger said. "Claire is right. We're not prepared to take on a killer. Think about what he did to Leann."

Maggie shuddered as she remembered the still form of the young woman, a life ended too soon because of a madman.

"You're right," Maggie said.

The three of them backed toward the door, keeping the room in full view at all times. They were almost free and clear, and the door was in reach, when a high-pitched wail cut through the quiet like a ragged blade, making all three of them jump and grab one another.

"That was a cry for help," Maggie said. "He's got someone."

She didn't hesitate. She broke ranks and rushed to the back, grabbing the only weapon she could find on the way— the stapler sitting on the front desk.

She shoved open the door to Sam's office, ready to do some damage. It was empty. She spun around to see Ginger and Claire crowded in the doorway, offering backup against their better judgment.

"I know I heard someone in here," Maggie said.

The three of them stood frozen, listening. The wail sounded again, and this time Claire frowned.

"That sounds like . . ." Her voice trailed off as she turned and went across the hall to the interview room.

She shoved open the door and leapt back. Maggie and Ginger peered around the door frame. The room was empty except for a battered table and chairs.

A noise sounded from under the table, and Maggie felt her whole body go tense just as a small gray cat jumped up onto the table. He blinked at them under the bright fluorescent lights and then began to lick his chest. It was Marshall Dillon.

"It's a cat!" Claire exclaimed, and she slumped against the doorjamb.

"He's Sam's cat," Maggie said. "Meet Marshall Dillon."

She crossed the room and held out her hand for him to sniff. He rubbed the side of his face against the back of her fingers in approval, and Maggie commenced with the scratching.

"Really?" Ginger asked. "I always saw Sam as more of a dog guy."

"The cat chooses the human," Maggie said.

"Ah," Ginger nodded in understanding. "Sam was adopted."

"He said Marshall likes to hang out at the station sometimes," Maggie said. "Today must have been one of those days."

"He sure is a handsome fella," Claire said. She was a certified cat lover.

Maggie scratched his favorite spot just under his chin, and when he started to purr, she felt all of her tension evaporate.

"Well, I'm sure glad the noise turned out to be a few pounds of annoyed cat and not a few hundred pounds of psychotic male," Ginger said.

The door slammed behind them, and Maggie whirled around to find Blake Caulfield standing there in his camel-colored coat, blocking the only exit.

Maggie felt her heart drop to her feet, dragging all of the blood in her body with it.

"By that, Mrs. Lancaster, I assume you mean me," Blake said.

Ginger leveled him with a glare, and Claire moved herself in front of Marshall Dillon.

"What are you doing here, Blake?" Maggie asked. "You know the police are looking for you."

"Yes, I'm aware," he said dryly. "Their timing really ruined my plans for the evening."

Maggie felt her throat constrict. "By that, you mean your plan to kill my daughter?"

"That would be the one," he confirmed. His eyes glinted with wicked malice.

"Why?" Maggie asked. "Why would you harm Laura? She's done nothing to you."

She began to lean in to Claire in a not-so-subtle push to get all of them away from Blake. The only barrier in the room was the table, and Maggie felt it was imperative to have it between him and them.

Ginger and Claire seemed to catch on and began to slowly inch away from him. Maggie stayed in front of the table while the others moved. She noticed Claire nudging Marshall Dillon down into one of the seats where he'd be out of sight. Once they were clear, she scooted around the table after them.

Blake had one hand in his pocket, and Maggie assumed it was a knife or a gun and that his intent was to do harm. If Blake had come here instead of running, he had to be pretty desperate or angry, neither of which left Maggie with a good feeling.

"Why?" he asked. "Because Laura ruined everything."

He looked at Maggie as if she were too stupid to live,

which at any other time would have offended her to the core. At the moment, however, her need to survive this encounter dominated any other feelings, drowning out her ability to process anything but terror.

"Do you have any idea how long I spent romancing Leann?" he asked. "Months. I spent months following her, learning her schedule, discovering what she liked to eat and where she liked to go. And then she vanished on me," Blake said.

The anger in his voice was palpable, and Maggie felt Claire and Ginger pause. She knew she had to prod him to keep his attention on her.

"That's not romancing someone, Blake; that's stalking," Maggie said. "Didn't you ever wonder why she vanished?"

"Shut up!" he shouted, and they all jumped. "I was not stalking her. I was doing research, making sure she was the one."

His cheeks flamed hot, and he looked agitated. Maggie felt Ginger give her arm a squeeze, and Maggie knew she was telling her to be careful.

"Yes, she moved here and took a different name, because of him," Blake snarled. "Not to get away from me, but because he wanted her to do it."

"He who?" Maggie asked. She was pleased that her voice sounded calm, because inside she was shaking like a leaf in a windstorm.

"You know who—Michael Claramotta," Blake snapped.

"You think Michael made her change her name?" Maggie asked.

"I know it," Blake said. "I overheard Leann's boss, Brody, tell her all about Michael Claramotta in Virginia and how he would help her out."

"How did you overhear it?" Maggie asked. She leaned in to Ginger to get the other two women moving again.

"Please." Blake gave her another condescending glance. "Bugging an office in a deli is child's play."

Suddenly, it all made sense, and Maggie stared at him in horror when she realized what else he had done. "It was you, wasn't it? You're the one who filed the restraining order against Michael. How?"

"I'm a clerk for the court," he said. "Creating a paper trail is pretty easy when you know how, and I knew it would make him look guilty of killing her, which is no more than he deserved for taking away the woman I loved."

"But why kill her?" Maggie asked. "If you loved her, why kill her?"

"Because she was doing it again," he said. He kept his hand in his pocket but ran the other through his hair in frustration. "She was making friends and going out. I worked so hard to get her all to myself, and that stupid butcher and your dumb daughter ruined it."

His rant ended on a high-pitched keen that made Maggie wince and tighten up as if he were about to hit her. He didn't. Instead, he looked across the room, past Maggie, as if he was seeing something that the rest of them couldn't.

"Don't you see?" he asked. "She was my soul mate. That's why I wanted to know everything about her before I approached her. And I did. I knew what books she read, what movies she went to, who her friends were and where she shopped. I wanted to show her how perfect we would be together."

"That's just creepy," Ginger said.

"It is not!" Blake yelled. "It's research. Knowledge is power, you know."

Maggie felt Ginger tremble beside her, and she reached down and grabbed Ginger's hand with her own. She squeezed her fingers to give her reassurance. Ginger squeezed back to let her know she was okay.

"How did you meet her?" Claire asked. Her voice was soft, and Maggie knew she was too scared to speak above a whisper, but it worked, because Blake seemed calmed by her tone, and he visibly relaxed.

"She came into the office where I work to pay a traffic ticket," he said. "She was very naughty and got ticketed for speeding. But then she smiled at me, and that's when I knew that she was the woman I was going to spend my life with. She was so beautiful. I knew I had to make her mine."

Maggie glanced at Ginger and Claire. Marshall Dillon hadn't moved from his chair but instead was crouched below the table edge as if he knew that Blake Caulfield was dangerous. Smart cat.

Blake met Maggie's gaze and smiled. He knew she was scared, and he was enjoying it. He thought he had them at his mercy, and Maggie realized that was all he'd ever wanted, to be the one who had the power. He'd wanted it over Leann, and he'd tried the same with Laura. If Sam hadn't gotten to her in time, he would have killed her. Maggie felt a surge of rage at what might have happened.

"Well, that didn't really work out for you, now, did it, Blake?" Maggie asked, knowing full well she was baiting him.

She saw Ginger flinch and knew her tone had been harsh,

but Maggie was tired of playing. Blake had them cornered in this tiny room, and it was getting hot. She could feel the sweat beading at her temples, and her breath was getting tight.

She didn't like the look on Blake's face. He looked smarmy and so sure of himself. It made her feel like a spider was scurrying across her skin.

"No, it didn't!" Blake snapped. "But that's okay, because I'm going to make everyone who kept her from me pay."

"We didn't keep her from you," Maggie said.

"Yes, you did!" Blake yelled. "I had Leann ready to accept me. She was new in town. She had no friends. And then your daughter shows up, and the next thing I know Leann is going out for coffee and wearing new clothes and makeup, and dancing at balls with other men!"

His face was red, and he was huffing and puffing as if every cell in his body were consumed with rage. He took his hand out of his pocket and Maggie almost sagged with relief when she saw that it was empty. He fisted his hands in his hair as he glared at them.

"I had to kill her, don't you see?" he cried. "She wasn't doing what she was supposed to do. She wasn't under my control anymore, and it's all because of your daughter. Laura just couldn't let well enough alone, could she?"

Maggie knew now was the moment. If Sam was bringing Laura here, Maggie would much rather be the one harmed by this lunatic than let him have another crack at her daughter.

She whipped her head at Ginger and Claire, and shouted, "Tackle now!"

Blake realized their intent, and his hand shot back into his pocket. Without his arm to brace him, he fell to the floor hard when Claire hit him from the side, Ginger took him out at the knees and Maggie gouged him with an elbow right in the chest. The tussle was messy. There were too many bodies, and Maggie knew she and the others were holding back for fear of hurting each other. Their hesitancy cost them.

Blake began kicking viciously and managed to clip Claire in the jaw with the toe of his shoe, sending her sprawling backward. Ginger went to sit on his legs, but with his free hand he punched her hard right in the temple.

Ginger staggered and Maggie cried out, even as she tried to subdue Blake by grabbing his arm. But three middle-aged bargain hunters were no match for a young man fueled by psychotic rage. Before Maggie could get a good grip on him, he had the sharp edge of a lethal looking knife pointed right at her throat.

Chapter 26

"Stop!" Blake shouted.

Maggie froze. Ginger and Claire, who had regrouped and were about to jump back into the fray, held their positions.

"Get up!" Blake said to Maggie, and then he turned to the others, and said, "Get back against the wall."

Maggie rose slowly to her feet while Ginger and Claire scooted back.

"You're coming with me," Blake said to Maggie. "If either of you interfere, I'll cut her."

He turned the knife, letting the overhead light shine down on its blade. Ginger swallowed and nodded, and Claire let out a small whimper. They both looked at Maggie with wide, frightened eyes.

Maggie gave them a small nod, letting them know they should do what he'd said. She couldn't have borne it if anything had happened to her friends.

Blake opened the door. He gestured with the knife for Maggie to lead the way. "After you—ah!"

Maggie jumped as Blake let out a high-pitched shriek. He dropped the knife and began spinning, as if trying to reach something on his back. Maggie kicked the knife through the open door and out of the room.

Ginger and Claire jumped to their feet and, as Blake whirled around yet again, Maggie saw a small ball of gray fur digging into the center of Blake's back for all he was worth. Marshall Dillon had disarmed a killer.

Blake seemed to catch on that it was an animal on his back, and he turned his back to the wall and looked like he was going to slam backward into the concrete to dislodge the cat. Maggie jumped between him and the wall, lifting her knee to block him. He tried to slam against her, but she didn't move her leg and used his nearness to snatch the cat off of his back.

Blake was shoved forward off her knee, and Claire cracked him on the head and back with one of the interrogation room chairs. Blake hit the ground with a sickly smack, his forehead bearing the brunt of the impact. Ginger put her foot on his back while Claire loomed over him with the chair, ready to hit him again.

Blake didn't move. Maggie hugged Marshall Dillon close, and he rubbed the top of his head under her chin. She had no doubt that the kitten had saved her life.

"What do we do—?" Ginger began, but a ruckus sounded from the front of the station house, interrupting her.

"Maggie!" Sam called. "Maggie, where are you?"

"Back here!" she cried. She would have run out to greet

him, but her legs were shaking, and she didn't think she had the strength.

"What are you doing?" Sam asked as he entered the room. He took the scene in at a glance, and then he visibly paled. "Are you all right?"

They all nodded. Sam stepped forward and checked Blake. Maggie could see that he was breathing, but he had a rapidly growing knot on his temple. With a head injury, it wasn't safe to move him. Sam seemed okay with that as he reached for his cuffs and secured Blake's hands behind his back.

Sam stood up and gestured for Claire to put the chair down. She seemed to have forgotten that she was holding it and lowered it quickly, letting it bang off the linoleum floor.

"Everything all right, Sheriff?" Deputy Dot Wilson poked her head in, and then she gasped.

"Deputy, keep an eye on him until the paramedics get here," Sam said.

"Yes, sir." Dot stepped into the room and took up a post out of reach of Blake and in between him and the door.

"If he comes to, call me," Sam said. "Ladies, let's get you out of here. Maggie, I've got a young lady outside who is pretty anxious to see her mom."

"Is she okay?" Maggie asked.

"She's fine," he said. "Shaken up but otherwise fine."

Sam gestured for them to leave, and Ginger and Claire practically ran him down, so eager were they to get out of the room of terror. As Maggie went to walk by him, Sam caught her in a quick hug that included Marshall Dillon. He kissed her head and exhaled a huge sigh.

"You're aging me, Maggie Gerber," he said.

"Just be glad you brought your fuzzy deputy in with you today," Maggie said. "Marshall Dillon attacked Blake when he was going to take me away as his new plaything. He—" Maggie's voice cracked, and she had to clear her throat before she could continue. "He saved my life."

"Did he, now?" Sam said. He scooped the kitten out of Maggie's arms and clutched him close with one hand while he put his other arm around Maggie and locked her against his side. "I think he's going to have to be officially deputized, then."

"It's the least you can do," Maggie said. "I really think he has a promising career in law enforcement."

Sam smiled, but then his gaze met Maggie's in a look that was equal parts fear and relief. He pulled her close and kissed her as if he was afraid it might be his last chance. Maggie grabbed his shirtfront and pulled him in even closer. She didn't want to think about the fact that she might never have gotten to kiss Sam or be this close to him again.

When they finally broke apart, Sam pressed his forehead against hers, and said, "You know, now that I've got you, I'm never going to let you go."

Maggie grinned. "I think you've got that backward. I'm the one who is never going to let you go."

Sam blinked at her, and a small smile played on his lips and spread into a full-on grin as their words created the new promise between them.

"Whoa, whoa, whoa," he said, still grinning. "I'm not the one who cut and ran all those years ago."

"Huh!" Maggie scoffed, her grin mirroring his. "Who

left for college and never bothered to find out why I dumped him?"

"Who did the dumping?" he countered.

They stared at each other as if they were about to engage in a tiff, but the blinding smiles on their faces made it clear that they couldn't be any happier to be giving each other a hard time.

Sam pulled her close and kissed her again. "It's never going to be boring with you around, is it?"

"Nope, and I'm sure you'll keep me on my toes, too," she said.

"I love you, Maggie."

"I love you, too, Sam."

At five o'clock on the dot on Christmas Eve, there was a knock on Maggie's front door. Maggie's mother and sister had arrived earlier in the day and were on the sunporch playing with Josh and visiting with Jake. Meanwhile, Maggie, Sandy and Laura were in the kitchen fixing the holiday dinner.

It was toasty warm in the kitchen, and Maggie was happy to excuse herself to go answer the door and feel the cold air on her face. Well, that and she was longing to see Sam. The arrest of Blake Caulfield had taken up all of his time over the past two days and, other than hurried phone calls, she hadn't seen or heard from him at all.

Blake Caulfield had been arrested for the murder of Leann Winthrop, the assault on Michael Claramotta, the kidnapping of Laura Gerber and the attempted kidnapping of Maggie Gerber, as well as the assaults on Claire Freemont and Ginger Lancaster. Sam was quite certain that Blake was never going to see daylight again.

Maggie opened the door, and there stood Sam. A light snow had begun earlier and was still coming down, coating his brown hair and clinging to his eyelashes. He had a bottle of wine in one hand and a bouquet of calla lilies in the other.

"Are those for me?" Maggie asked as she pulled him inside and shut the door behind him.

"The wine is," he said. He leaned down and gave her a quick kiss on the lips. "But the flowers are for your mother."

"Oh, really?"

"Hey, if I want permission to keep dating her daughter, I know I need to get in good with your mom."

"Indeed," Maggie said. She was more than a little nervous about her mother's reaction to Sam.

"Well, if it isn't Sam Collins," a voice said from across the room.

Maggie glanced over her shoulder to see her mother standing in the doorway, staring daggers through her bifocals at Sam. Lizzie O'Brien was a compact version of Maggie and her older sister. Her red hair had long since gone to white, and she wore it in a topknot on her head. She dressed in comfy slacks and tailored blouses and always accessorized with a nice piece of jewelry. She might be pushing seventy, but Maggie had no doubt that she could take Sam if she put her mind to it. Because if there was one thing that got her mother's temper up, it was someone who messed with her family.

"Now, Mom," Maggie began.

"Don't you 'Now, Mom' me," her mother said.

Maggie looked back at Sam and gave him an apologetic smile, but her mother kept right on going.

"You broke my baby's heart," Lizzie said to Sam. "Now, what do you have to say for yourself?"

Sam looked her square in the eye and said, "I'm sorry."

"Huh." Lizzie didn't sound impressed.

"Mom, I told you it wasn't Sam's fault," Maggie said. "Summer Phillips fooled me into thinking that it was him she was fooling around with, but it wasn't."

Lizzie tipped her head back and studied Sam through her glasses, clearly not satisfied.

"It's true," Sam said. "But I should have demanded to know why Maggie refused to see me."

Lizzie's eyebrows lifted, and her face cleared a bit. "Well, you did save my granddaughter from a maniac, and you appear to be learning to communicate."

Sam and Maggie waited while she studied them, and Maggie abruptly felt like she had just gone back in time about twenty years. Ridiculous.

"Are those flowers for me?" Lizzie asked.

"Yes, ma'am," he said, and stepped forward to hand them to her.

"Thank you," Lizzie said, and gave him a small smile. "Looks like you're staying for dinner. Don't you think you should be serving soon, Maggie?"

"It'll be just a few more minutes, Mom," Maggie said. "Maybe you could tell everyone to wash up?"

Lizzie studied them both for a moment and then gave them a warning look. "Just remember, Sam Collins, I have my eye on you."

She turned and left the room. Sam gave Maggie a concerned look.

"Does that mean she approves?" he asked.

"Well, she didn't toss you out into the snow," Maggie said, "so, we'll just cling to that victory for now."

"I'd rather cling to you," Sam said. He put the wine down and pulled her close, and then he kissed her like he meant it.

As if by mutual agreement, no one spoke about the horror of the past few days during dinner. Talk was kept light and teasing as everyone watched Josh get more and more excited for the coming morning. Maggie glanced around the table, studying the faces of everyone she loved and gave silent thanks that they were all here together.

Jake and Sandy were just taking Josh to bed when the faint sound of singing came from outside. Maggie went to the front door to peer out, and there in front of her house were the GBGs and all of their families—Claire and Pete, Joanne and Michael, Ginger and Roger and all four of their boys—as well as Bianca and Max and, in a happy surprise, Doc and Alice Franklin.

Josh hurried to the front door and his round little face split into a grin as he joined in with his favorite song, about a red-nosed reindeer. When it was over, Maggie ushered everyone into the house for cookies and cocoa.

The small house was now full to bursting with people. Michael and Joanne were talking to Jake and Sandy while they watched Josh with the wonder of being new parents. Pete and Claire were in the kitchen with Max and Bianca making more cocoa for everyone. Laura and the Lancaster boys had taken over the living room and were watching *It's a Wonderful Life*. Maggie's mother was talking with Doc and Alice while Maggie's sister chatted with Ginger and Roger, and Maggie noted that the six of them frequently gave Maggie and Sam knowing looks. Whatever.

When Sam slipped his arm around her shoulders and pulled her close, he whispered in her ear, "Are you all right?"

"Never better," Maggie said.

She didn't know what the future held for her and Sam, for her daughter or for any of the GBGs. But if the past week had taught her anything, it was to be grateful for the perfect moments, like this one, for they were what made life worth living.

Money Saving Holiday Tips

Maggie likes to send holiday cards to all of her friends, but since she is a single mom and now owns a small business, she has to get the most bang for her postal buck so she sends festive holiday postcards that she creates by cutting regular holiday cards, that she bought on sale after the previous Christmas, in half and mailing them as postcards.

Joanne loves to decorate for the holidays and she does it by bringing the outdoors inside. Pinecones and pine boughs, which make the house smell wonderful, as well as holly berries and dried vines are all favorites for the mantel piece as well the table centerpiece.

Claire loves to send gifts to her family, who live far away, but she also wants to make it personal, so she and the Good Buy Girls get together with several of their friends and have a cookie exchange. Each of the participants bakes a dozen of one type of cookie for each person attending. Once the exchange is done, Claire has enough to send to her family as gifts.

Ginger has four growing boys to feed and the holidays give her plenty of opportunities to save money on groceries. When buying produce, she always makes sure it's dry. Vegetables that have been sprayed with water weigh more and cost more. Also, when her boys don't eat every bit of meat and vegetables, she takes what's left in the serving dishes and scrapes them into a one gallon sealable bucket that she keeps in her freezer. When it's full, she puts it in a big pot with some canned tomatoes or broth along with some cooked cubed chicken or beef and makes a hearty soup.

Maggie has lived in St. Stanley her entire life and her list of people to give gifts is almost as long as the phone book. The most economical way for her to give gifts to everyone is to make them herself. Her favorite gift to give is a consumable gift. To fight off the winter's chilly weather she recommends hot chocolate.

Maggie's Go-To Gift: Hot Chocolate for Two

You will need (per gift):

1 pint-sized canning jar with lid (clean and dry)
½ cup sugar
½ cup unsweetened cocoa powder
½ cup powdered milk
Pinch of salt

Crushed peppermint candy (optional for peppermint
  cocoa)
Mini marshmallows

Layer sugar, cocoa, powdered milk, and salt in jar. Next layer peppermint (optional) and marshmallows. Seal the jar with the lid. Now decorate the jar with the ribbons and bows of your choice. Lastly, add a decorative tag with the instructions: Mix contents in a medium pot with 2 ⅔ cups boiling water. Makes 2 servings.

Happy Holidays from the Good Buy Girls!

Read below for a preview of
Josie Belle's next Good Buy Girls Mystery . . .

Marked Down for Murder

Coming soon from Berkley Prime Crime!

"More flowers?" Ginger Lancaster asked as she walked into My Sister's Closet, her best friend's secondhand store, behind Henry Dawson, the local florist. Joanne Claramotta and Claire Freemont followed right behind her.

The women belonged to a self-named group called the Good Buy Girls. They were friends who were all about bargain hunting and thrift, and since Maggie had opened her shop, it had become the hub of their operation and their unofficial meeting place.

"Yep, she's got another one," Henry said. "Looks like someone's got quite the admirer."

For the past three days, Henry had delivered a single red rose to Maggie Gerber with a card with one word on it. Maggie took the rose from Henry and felt her face grow warm. She was embarrassed but also a bit giddy from the attention.

"Thank you so much," she said. She tried to offer him a tip but he waved her away.

"You keep your money, Maggie," he said. "I've been paid more than enough."

Maggie gave him a chagrinned look and his wrinkled, old face split into a smile that showed off his dentures.

"Well, don't hold back," Joanne said. "What's the word of the day?"

Maggie put the red rose in a vase with two others and opened the small card. The word *You* was scrawled in a blocky script in a black felt-tip pen. She knew that handwriting. It belonged to her boyfriend, Sam Collins, who happened to be the police chief of St. Stanley, their small Virginia town. Of course when she had questioned him the previous two days, he had denied all knowledge of any flowers or cards.

When put together in order the cards read, *Maggie, Will You.*

"Squee!" Joanne let out a squeal. Her long brown ponytail swung back and forth as she bounced up and down on her feet.

"That is just the most romantic gesture ever," Claire sighed. She pushed her black rectangular glasses up on her nose. "I wonder what he's going to ask you."

"I don't know," Henry said. "But I'm betting I'll see you tomorrow and every day right up until Valentine's Day."

Maggie and the others waved to him as he left the shop. Ginger turned back to face Maggie and rested her chin on her hand as she leaned on the counter and studied the cards.

"So, what do you think he's going to ask you?" Her teeth

flashed white against her brown skin and her dark eyes gleamed with delight.

"I don't know," Maggie said. "I keep asking him, but he keeps denying that it's him."

Ginger's eyebrows rose. "Do you think it's someone else?"

"No," Maggie said. "I recognize the handwriting."

"Don't freak out on me," Claire said. "But do you think he's going to propose?"

"No!" Maggie said. "No, no, no."

"Well, don't beat around the bush," Ginger said. "Tell us how you feel."

"We've only been dating for two months, not even, a proposal would be . . ."

"Romantic?" Joanne sighed and the others did, too.

"I was thinking premature," Maggie said. She frowned at them. "Besides, logically speaking it doesn't work."

"What do you mean?" Ginger asked.

Maggie leaned toward the cards and a hank of her auburn hair fell over her face. She tucked it behind her ear as she tapped the counter with her index finger.

"There are four more days to Valentine's Day," she said. "So if he did have a rose and a card delivered every day then a proposal really wouldn't work because *marry* and *me* would only be two more days."

"Unless he's planning something even more spectacular for the next two days," Joanne said. She started jumping up and down again and Ginger put an arm around her.

"Settle down girl," she said. "You are going to jiggle that baby right out."

Joanne instantly put her hands on her belly and her eyes grew wide. "You think so?"

"No," Ginger said as she gave her a half hug. "I'm just teasing."

"How long now?" Claire asked.

"I'm eight months give or take a few days," Joanne said. "My OB says it could be anytime if the baby decides to come early."

"A baby," Maggie sighed. "It seems like ages since I've held a newborn."

"So, if you and Sam do get married, will you have another baby?" Claire asked.

"I . . . uh . . . huh?" Maggie stammered. "Sorry, I think I just swallowed my tongue."

Ginger hooted with laughter. "You could, you know."

"Yeah, you're still young enough," Joanne said. "Just think, our babies would be close enough in age to play together."

"Aw," Claire said. "That would be so cute."

Maggie glanced at Claire. "Don't you start. You and Pete could get married and have kid, too, you know."

Claire shook her head. "No, that's not in the cards for me. I knew long ago that I was not mother material. My cat, Mr. Tumnus, is all the dependent I can handle, thank you very much."

"Is Pete okay with that?" Joanne asked.

"Yes," Claire said. "We had a long frank talk when we first started dating and we both decided that parenting was not our calling, so it looks like it's all on Maggie and you, unless of course Ginger wants to try again for a girl."

"Oh, gracious, no," Ginger said. "Four boys are all I can handle, besides after Dante came along, I had them take out all of my plumbing since it had begun to collapse. So, it's just Maggie then."

Maggie put a hand to her forehead as a sudden attack of woozy hit her like a freight train. Did Sam want kids? She had no idea. They'd never discussed it.

The bells on the front door jangled and Maggie glanced up, willing someone, anyone to arrive and save her from this conversation.

The woman who arrived was not her first or even her last pick but times being desperate she decided not to quibble.

"Summer Phillips," Maggie cried. She came around the counter and greeted the woman who had been her lifelong nemesis with a wide warm smile. "Come in, how are you, dear?"

Summer froze in mid-step. She looked at Maggie as if she was worried that she was ill with something that could be contagious and deadly.

"What's wrong with you?" Summer asked. She tossed her long, bottle-bleached hair over her shoulder and held out a well-manicured hand to ward Maggie off.

"Not a thing," Maggie lied. "I'm just being neighborly. What can I do for you, Summer?"

"She's panicking," Ginger whispered to Claire and Joanne, and Maggie heard them all giggle.

"Nothing," Summer said. "I don't want anything from you."

A woman nudged into the shop behind Summer. She had the same pretty face as Summer, with an upturned nose and prominent cheekbones, but she was obviously older with very fine lines around her eyes and mouth. Her hair was cut in a dark brown bob and it swung about her face in graceful sweeps as she looked Maggie up and down.

"Mom, this is Maggie Gerber," Summer said. She stood aside and crossed her arms over her chest.

"Your mother?" Maggie asked. She glanced at the woman still scrutinizing her. Yes, she vaguely remembered Summer's mother, Blair Phillips, from their high school days but she knew Blair had been married at least three times since then and she had no idea what her name was now.

Blair's lips pursed to the side and her eyes narrowed. Then she shook her head. "No, no, I refuse to believe it. There is absolutely no way that Sam Collins threw you over for *this*."